I0629823

ADAM B. WILSON & ALEXANDRA K. DAEMICKE

CADAVER CHRONICLES

The Code of Silence

SUPERIOR
OBLIQUE
PUBLISHING

Superior Oblique Publishing
34 West Roberta Street
Lemont, IL 60439

Published in the United States by Superior Oblique Publishing.
First Edition, June 2023.

Front Cover*: AI-Generated Image. "Award-winning photo in the style of Gunther Frank von Hagen, anatomy of a male face, view front of the face, view muscles, black background" prompt. Midjourney, Inc, San Francisco, CA, 16 May. 2023. midjourney.com/app/.

*This artistic representation does not accurately depict anatomical structures.

Back Cover: AI-Generated Image. "Paper origami swan, simple, not complex, white paper, black background" prompt. Midjourney, Inc, San Francisco, CA, 20 May. 2023. midjourney.com/app/.

ISBN: 979-8-9884365-0-8 (eBook)

ISBN: 979-8-9884365-1-5 (paperback)

ISBN: 979-8-9884365-2-2 (hardcover)

To my beloved children, Mackenzie Sawyer and Hank Elliot. May you one day grow to realize the power and potential of your imagination. Love, Dad.

To my wife, Megan, for always supporting my endeavors.

Adam B. Wilson

To my parents, who have been my best guides in life. Thank you for your endless love and support.

To my husband, Ricky, who is my rock. Thank you for treating my aspirations as if they are your own.

To my son, Owen, who is the light of my life. May your light ignite an endless curiosity to learn and a passion to chase after your dreams.

Alexandra K. Daemicke

CADAVER CHRONICLES

The Code of Silence

CHAPTER 1

CODE GRAY

Galen's slumped-over body lay limp and motionless in the hospital's rear stairwell. He was hardly conscious. The cinder block wall supported his weight, and his accomplice, Tome, gripped his arm to steady his balance. He landed two inches shy of brutally plummeting to the lower landing. Galen's physical body could no longer bear the misery of the transformation's intensity. The agonizing loss of his former self, and the adrenaline surge inherent in any covert mission, brought Galen to his breaking point. The subtle, yet precarious, rise and fall of his breathless chest put Tome on edge. Uncertain whether to slap his cheeks or to douse him with cold water, Tome pried open Galen's palpebral fissures with his toothpick-like fingers. Galen's eyes beat with uncontrolled nystagmus, a hopeful sign his languor would be short-lived.

"Code gray! Code gray!" shouted Dr. Floundary between breaths. He raced through the unit's corridor to the nurses' station. The tails of his white coat fluttered wildly behind him as a drag of air countered his forward velocity. A postcard-sized flyer, sloppily tucked in his coat's side pocket, jostled free. It sank to the floor like an emu's feather. Furrowed brows accentuated his acute focus and brood demeanor.

The head charge nurse lowered steaming coffee from her pursed lips at the sound of Dr. Floundary's commotion. Instinctively, her delicate fingers pranced on the keyboard like two dancers competing for a solo. Her eyes zigzagged across the monitor from one icon to another to initiate the protocol.

Within seconds, three ascending chimes rang out over the intercom. An automated female voice in an artificial tone announced, "Your attention, please. Code gray. Cardiac unit. Seventh floor." The flat monotone voice repeated itself once more.

Back in the stairwell, Galen sluggishly regained consciousness. Though lethargic, he mustered enough strength to begin the long descent down the seven flights of stairs. Tome followed in line behind him keeping a close watch as Galen sporadically faltered from one flight to the next. Galen's throbbing head and blurry vision only complicated their exit slowing their escape.

"What did he look like?" demanded Dr. Floundary, leaning over the nurses' workstation like an incessant interrogator.

"Who?" asked the flustered charge nurse. She inched her rolling chair backward to reclaim her bubble of personal space. "And why did I just initiate an emergency security request?" The buzz of her smartwatch vibrated against her wrist. Though physically fit and typically calm under fierce pressure, her heart rate had just exceeded 100 beats per minute.

"The one you called my research assistant," answered Dr. Floundary, pacing down the unit's corridor for any sign of an intruder, "what did he look like? Which direction did he head?" His foot unexpectedly slid beneath him as he transferred his weight in the opposite direction. The smooth sole of his dress shoe compacted a pile of soot, momentarily losing all traction. "What the deuce is this mess?" Dr. Floundary's struggle to regain his composure was just as hollow as his attempt to foot-sweep the scattered ashes back into a pile.

"Is there an arsonist on the floor?" The charge nurse's concern grew as her thoughts spewed into words within earshot of other nurses who struggled to process Dr. Floundary's agitation.

"What do you remember about my *supposed* research assistant?" pressed Dr. Floundary. He meticulously dusted off his wingtips with a handkerchief in hand, leveraging the workstation's countertop for added balance.

The charge nurse stammered a wavering response, not expecting to begin her early morning shift with such distress or confusion. "He was darker-complected and of average height. He had a terrible nervous stutter." She stared over the counter at the unit's reception area, deep in thought. "It's possible he was not alone. He walked towards two other men after I gave him the patient's room number." She paused, not knowing if she had said too much. She internally questioned whether she could be held responsible for any wrongdoing that may have transpired with the information she disseminated. "But I don't know for certain if he was with them or not. When I returned from the breakroom with coffee, all three were gone." She hid her face behind cupped hands, feeling she had just been played like a fiddle in some elaborate scheme.

"And the others? What were their features? What were they wearing?" asked Dr. Floundary as he reclaimed the dropped postcard from the floor. He quickly hid the flyer advertising a white present wrapped with a red bow in the inner pocket of his lab coat ashamed of its contents.

"They were all wearing scrubs, but I don't recall what they looked like." The nurse walked around to the counter's front as if standing in their place would help her to remember. "One of the Caucasian gentlemen looked older. He had saggy skin. The other was possibly anemic. He was as pale as a porcelain China doll." She paused again. "And they were all bald!" Odd, she thought, realizing her observation.

"Great, so we're looking for three bald thugs. Were any of them packing heat?" he flippantly asked.

Dazed by the thought of concealed handguns and being an unknown accomplice, the charge nurse's skin prickled with horror. As a poised woman, she stood perfectly still, almost submissively, with her hands folded neatly in front of her. While she recognized Dr. Floundary was not directing his diminutive tirade at her, she was overly cautious not to provoke him.

"That's not much to go on," blurted Dr. Floundary with deflated enthusiasm. He rubbed the back of his neck, straining to think as he paced.

Two security personnel emerged from the elevator. "Who initiated the code gray?"

"I did!" Dr. Floundary spoke first. "There is at least one individual who needs to be detained and possibly two accomplices."

More security personnel flooded onto the floor. One emerged from the rear stairwell, and two more careened from the second elevator.

A large burly man inserted himself into the center of the conversation. His rolled-up uniform sleeves were so tight they were choking his bulging biceps. "What's the situation?" he ordered, gluing his dominant hand to his Glock holster.

Dr. Floundary immediately asserted his authority, "Someone is illegally impersonating a medical professional."

"Did you directly observe this?" asked the weightlifting brute in the skin-tight uniform. His eyes carefully tracked the restless Dr. Floundary, who had yet to settle himself.

"I'm certain of it," he stated emphatically. "The suspects are wearing scrubs and have alopecia." The security personnel exchanged sideways glances. "Two are Caucasian; the third is a darker skin tone."

"They're bald," interjected the charge nurse. The officers nodded.

A lean, clean-shaven patrolman wearing yellow sporty eyewear and heavy work boots led with his shoulder as he wedged himself through the tight closed-off circle of officers. "I just passed two bald men in scrubs at level three in the rear stairwell."

The dominant brawny officer cocked his head and engaged the radio's call button pinned to his shoulder. His excessively thick neck made his ears look childlike in comparison. "Lockdown the building!"

"Spread out. We must find them," barked Dr. Floundary in a way his coworkers had never seen before. He exuded steadfast determination to secure the suspects. It was personal.

CHAPTER 2

IN LIMBO

Several days earlier.

The sun broke over the eastern corner of the Heidelberg bell tower. Tree canopies swayed in the wind as if treasuring the tower's ringing chimes. Lines of nautical flags reached from the tops of quaint nearby storefronts to the lampposts flanking the banks of the Neckar.

The sweltering sun reflected intensely off the murky water and beautifully lit the grandiose archways supporting the town's landmark sandstone bridge. Old Bridge, as it was commonly called, marked the start and the end of the two-mile longboat race.

The crowd grew steadily in anticipation of the opening ceremony. Spectators gathered in droves for the town's acclaimed Heidelberg Regatta. Loyal citizens and alumni, donned in university-lettered apparel, secured their spots on the inclines of the grassy embankments among friends and curious travelers. The onlookers welcomed the relief of a water-cooled breeze. Students flocked to the water's edge to cheer on their fellow classmen. With handmade signs and painted faces, the lively crowd captured the essence of local town pride in every way.

One inauspicious student lifted a coconut-sized stone overhead. He pounded a bronze-colored flagpole into the embankment like a proletarian driving an iron spike through a railroad tie. The Heidelberg University seal embellished the center of the wool flag and overlaid three vertical bands denoting the country's signature stripes. The flag's unruly marshal stretched it taught until the flaccid pennant could seize the next gust. Pointing to the crest, he howled lewd remarks and vulgarities to the crowd opposite the Neckar.

As the tower's bell ended its ninth resounding ring, the master of ceremonies approached a wooden podium embossed with the town's historical coat of arms. The insignia, showcasing a crowned lion, drew onlookers' attention to the center of the makeshift stage. The crowd quieted to a soft murmur awaiting the customary greeting. The announcer approached the podium wearing a garnet red blazer over a white twill button-down shirt with a cognac leather belt. His frosted goatee added balance to his navy blue-rimmed frames. After shuffling a pile of loose papers caught unexpectedly by the wind, the announcer adjusted the microphone and began.

"Welcome to the 96th annual Heidelberg Regatta! A famous novelist once wrote, 'A man who lives fully is prepared to die at any time.'"

Individuals in the crowd shared glances of confusion. Some competitors even settled their oars to listen with greater attentiveness. "While he may not have anticipated his death," the announcer paused to clear his throat, "the young life of Gavin Hartmann was certainly well-lived and full of accomplishments. He was a friend to many, a passionate debater, and a rising regatta star. Gavin Hartmann was avidly pursuing a men's rowing scholarship at the University of Munich and often trained with the Heidelberg rowing team. Throughout his short life, he served our community as a member of the national honors society and, most recently, he volunteered countless hours to help revitalize our local library system." The announcer paused, readjusting his windblown comb-over. "As a highly ambitious, confidant, and well-liked 17-year-old, Gavin had significant potential to become the attorney he longed to be." The announcer glanced down to consult his sloppy handwritten script. "It is my solemn duty to inform you that, yesterday, a tragic accident suddenly took Gavin Hartmann's life. On behalf of myself and our community, I extend my deepest sympathy and heartfelt thoughts to his family and pray that something good will come from this tragic incident. In remembrance of Gavin and his exceptional character, let us observe a moment of silence."

The crowd gasped. No one foresaw hearing such tragic news on a day that promised comradery and memorable festivities. Over the next sixty sluggish seconds, the silence was punctuated only by the occasional splash of water breaking against the sides of the tethered longboats.

Two miles away from the regatta festivities in a Baroque-style building with a limestone façade, Gavin, too, observed silence. Except for a sporadic moan from a distant water pipe, Gavin heard only the faint stream of chilled air as it squeezed itself past a torn rubber gasket. A broken seal separated the metal table on which he laid from the stainless steel walls that encapsulated him. Gavin could not see his surroundings. A damp blue shroud enveloped his entire head. He felt a sheet draped on top of him from head to toe. As he rested motionless, waves of stupor overcame him. Gavin felt sedated as if undergoing a surgical procedure. Although conscious, he could not move his extremities or maneuver his jaw. His paralyzed muscles and joints entrapped him. No amount of concentration on even the simplest task could stimulate the contraction of a single myocyte.[1] No matter how much effort he put forth, he could not wrinkle his forehead, speak, or scratch the lingering itch on his thigh.

"If I could just remove this suffocating towel," Gavin ruminated with angst recalling the time one of his sisters triggered his claustrophobia by smothering him under a pillow. The prolonged mental anguish and confusion fully consumed and eventually subdued him. Hours, perhaps days, passed before Gavin regained consciousness. Yet to him, the renewal of his attentiveness occurred in what felt like a matter of minutes. He preemptively assumed his paralyzed condition was a grim transient dream until the feeling of the shroud stretched like

---

[1] A myocyte is a muscle cell.

a canvas over his anterior reminded him otherwise. As his apprehension grew like a compressing weight on his chest, he could no longer shake the image of a mummy enclosed by a metal coffin. The frenzied madness of his mind made him comatose to any awareness of space or time.

He drifted in and out of consciousness. During a late transitory state, Gavin felt gentle but deliberate tugs on his body from multiple directions. Like a marionette, a force manipulated him outside of his own will. The occasional prick of a needle in the oddest of locations brought him back from the depths of his wandering thoughts. The voices and conversations exchanged around him were mostly unintelligible. By chance, he heard the deep vocal timbre of a male instructing another, "Inscribe *Galen* on his nameplate." He fell back into unconsciousness at the sound of a constant slow-blowing stream of warm air.

At last, Gavin awoke drowsy, disoriented, and chilled to the core. The murmur of distant voices surrounded him. His hearing was muffled, and, at first, his joints moved with cogwheel rigidity. His muscles ached as though he had just completed a triathlon. Before another unbearable sensation could cross his mind, he felt an ice-cold hand press against his bare chest. The hand sternly shook his chest plate. "Galen! Galen! Wake up!"

Gavin Hartmann opened his eyes. His head was no longer wrapped in a shroud. He saw someone, or something, he had never seen before standing in front of him.

CHAPTER 3

THE AWAKENING

Gavin, feeling exposed, quickly sat upright from the floor. Instinctively, he positioned his hands as a shield in front of him and turned his head away in fear. He was reluctant to take another look.

With a scratchy tremble in his voice, he uttered, "Who are you? What do you want? If it's money you need, just take it. It's in my wallet. Here!"

Gavin reached blindly to extract the wallet from his pocket but was startled to realize he was not wearing pants. He glanced down at his arms and legs. Within seconds his eyelids fluttered shut. His eyes rolled upward into their sockets. He fainted.

Marcel, kneeling behind Gavin, caught his trunk as his body fell limp. Marcel mouthed to Cameo, who was the cause of Gavin's syncope, "Find something to prop his head."

After a blank stare, Cameo removed his own skin like doffing a trench coat and neatly folded it like linen cloth. Proud of his ingenuity, Cameo handed the makeshift bolster of integument to Marcel.

"I guess that will do," Marcel scoffed. He repositioned Gavin on the floor and ordered another body standing at Gavin's feet, "Alert Arden. We have a fainter."

Moments later, the orthogonal-looking body returned with Arden alongside. A crowd of bodies gathered up close to the platform to see the gangly newbie awkwardly sprawled in all his glory. Arden made his way through the pack and stepped up onto the display.

"Give Galen some room," Arden's voice bellowed to the onlookers.

Like regimented soldiers, those kneeling closest to the newcomer inched backward and stepped down off the platform placing their bare feet on the cool Carrara marble.

"We must wake him," Arden stated.

"Last time we had a fainter, we used burning bone," suggested Cameo. "No one can sleep through the smell of smoldering osteons.[2]"

"Very well," permitted Arden as he turned over his shoulder and called out to the crowd. "Ivory, can you lend us a hand?"

Ivory, gingerly ambulated toward the platform. She politely excused herself as she bumped shoulders with other curious bodies. She was nothing more than an upright walking pile of bones. She stood five-foot-six with thin metal wires laced meticulously between her joints.

---

[2] A single osteon looks like the cross-section of a tree trunk. Osteons are the basic functional units of compact bone made up of central (Haversian) canals, containing blood vessels, surrounded by concentric rings (lamellae) of matrix and bone cells (osteocytes) located within spaces called lacunae.

She looked like any other biology room skeleton, except she supported her own weight without any rolling suspension system. She carried herself like a sophisticated aristocrat adorned for an evening soirée. She wore a sapphire ring on her middle finger and pearls around her neck. A diamond-encrusted headband accented with a black feather snuggly encircled her cranium. Having granted this request before, Ivory casually unhinged the wires binding her wrist to her forearm. Like a relative passing butter at Thanksgiving, she gave Arden her entire disarticulated wrist and hand, from carpals to distal phalanges.[3] If this were not awkward enough, Ivory then removed her femur[4] from her pelvis's concaved acetabulum.[5]

Like a craftsman using fine sandpaper to smooth the rough carvings of a milled baseball bat, Arden wrapped Ivory's hand around her donated femur and vigorously chafed bone against bone with friction-producing force. It smelt like burnt powdered cheese puffs. The noxious scent instantly filled the air, unpleasantly stimulating the olfactory nerves[6] of those gathered nearby. Cameo knelt beside Gavin's head and, with outstretched palms, waved his hands like a confused mime as he directed the wafting aroma into Gavin's nares.[7]

---

[3] The eight carpal bones form the wrist. The metacarpals are the bones in the palm of the hand. The phalanges form the fingers. Each of the four fingers is comprised of proximal (closest to the wrist), middle, and distal (farthest from the wrist) phalanges. The thumb has only a proximal phalanx and distal phalanx.

[4] The femur is the thigh bone.

[5] The acetabulum is the large socket that articulates with the head of the femur. The femur and acetabulum represent the largest ball-and-socket joint in the body.

[6] The olfactory nerves are one of twelve pairs of cranial nerves. They are located in the roof of the nasal cavity and convey the sense of smell (olfaction) to the brain.

[7] The terms *nare* and *nostril* are synonymous.

Gavin came too with a violent sneeze and a subtle look of disgust. The look was all too familiar to Arden. Kneeling at Gavin's side, he firmly pressed the palm of his hand against Gavin's forehead, temporarily blinding him to his new environment. Before Gavin could utter a word, Arden introduced himself.

"My name is Arden. You were startled by the sight of my friend, who is called Cassius." Cassius spontaneously raised his hand to identify himself, though Gavin's eyes remained hidden beneath Arden's palm.

"Before I remove my hand from your brow, I must warn you that you are no longer who you once were. The world you are now in is very different from that which you have come." Distracted, Arden paused at the sight of Cameo shaking Ivory's disarticulated hand. "When you open your eyes, you will see the entrusted inhabitants of this world standing before you. We, including you, are the same. I will introduce you to your new comrades once you grapple with whom you have become. Do you understand?"

In a combination of fear and uncertainty, Gavin nodded as best he could under the pressure of Arden's palm. Arden slowly removed his hand from Gavin's brow. Gavin hesitantly lifted his eyelids to scan his surroundings. Human-like beings encircled him, standing in deadening silence. From his position on the platform, he could only see the upper torsos and heads of the beings in his field of view. The first row of inhabitants kneeled at the edge of the elevated platform while the second and third tiers of onlookers peered anxiously over their shoulders.

The beings looked remarkably lifelike. They were delicately preserved humans. Swallowing any saliva he had left, Gavin found the courage to partially erect himself. Propping himself to a fully seated position, Gavin panned the room from left to right as far as his neck would allow. To his rear, Arden authoritatively announced to the crowd, "Carry on with your evening. There will be plenty of time to meet Galen in the coming days."

Everyone scattered except for Cameo, Marcel, and Arden. Marcel stood over Gavin and extended his hand in a gesture of friendliness. Gavin took hold and rose to his feet from the hard glossy surface. He stared intently at Marcel, whose skin, like many others, was missing. He could tell Marcel was very athletic. His muscles, all exposed, were fit and shaped with impeccable contours. Artistically, Marcel's pectoralis major muscles flared laterally like wings from the sides of his chest.

Gavin then turned his attention to Cameo, whom he saw bend down out of the corner of his eye. In a state of wonderment, he watched Cameo as he shook out the wrinkles of the folded skin that had served as the pillow propping his head. Cameo was an average-sized man whose muscles were no rival to Marcel's. He hobbled gracelessly on one foot as he dressed in the unfurled skin as if it was a one-piece jumpsuit. The only thing missing was a zipper up the front.

Judging by the tone of his voice and his age-drawn face, Gavin knew that Arden was further along in years than the others. Arden, too, had been skinned. His platysma muscle,[8] reminiscent of wet, thinly shredded paper, was removed to reveal his anterior neck's infrahyoid muscles[9] coursing behind the insertion of his more prominent sternocleidomastoids.[10] A nickel chain, drawn downward by the weight of two dog tags, encircled the root of his neck. More notably, his partially removed calvarium exposed the left hemisphere of his well-vascularized brain. As if these vulnerabilities were not enough, the reflected masseter muscle[11] on the side of his face uncovered the healthy beige-colored bone of his lower jaw and the inferior alveolar nerve[12] coursing through it.

Finally, after finding a morsel of courage, Gavin spoke, "My name is Gavin Hartmann. Why are you calling me Galen?"

From the side of the platform, a bizarre-looking man of mostly bone and nerves popped up out of nowhere and said, "Galen. That's your name. That's what the nameplate says." As quickly as the man had appeared, he vanished. He scurried off to the other side of the room and disappeared behind a partially freestanding

---

[8] The platysma muscle is a paper-thin muscle of facial expression that overlies the sternocleidomastoid and infrahyoid muscles. The platysma muscle tenses the skin of the neck, such as during shaving.

[9] There are four infrahyoid muscles that primarily depress the hyoid bone and larynx (voice box) during swallowing and phonation.

[10] The sternocleidomastoid muscles run obliquely from the sternum (sterno-) and clavicle (cleido-) to the mastoid process (the bump behind the ear). This muscle primarily rotates the head contralaterally (to the side opposite of where the muscle is located) during unilateral contraction (when only one muscle contracts). Bilateral contraction (when both muscles contract) results in neck flexion.

[11] The masseter muscle is one of four muscles of mastication for chewing. The masseter elevates the mandible (the lower jaw) to forcibly close the mouth.

[12] The inferior alveolar nerve carries sensory information from the teeth and gums of the mandible and from the skin of the chin via its termination called the mental nerve.

wall.

"I assure you it is no mistake," Arden said. "And that was Vitalis. He is always jittery and full of life. As you may have noticed, he is a little light in the head."

Gavin had noticed. Vitalis, literally, had no brain. Only an inch-wide section down the middle of his skull remained like a bony Mohawk. Visible beneath the osseous strip were the superior sagittal sinus,[13] the falx cerebri,[14] and an empty cranial vault.

"He never thinks before he speaks," Arden grinned half-jokingly.

Gavin franticly interrupted, "What do you mean, it's not a mistake? I'm Gavin Hartmann. I live in Heidelberg with my three sisters and parents."

In his calm and collected demeanor, Arden replied, "Before I removed my hand, what did I say?"

"You said, 'You are no longer who you once were' and something about a different world, but I don't understand. What do you mean?" Gavin's tone became more and more demanding.

In his gallant voice, Arden recited his typical monolog. "We are neither ghosts, ghouls, nor goblins; nor are we angels or saints. We are not grotesque oddities, as some like to think. Never were we poor, tortured, or imprisoned." Arden began to walk, expecting Gavin to keep pace. "We are cadavers, dead, yet invaluable

---

[13] The superior sagittal sinus runs internally along the top midline of the skull, at the upper border of the falx cerebri. This sinus conveys venous blood from the brain and helps to return cerebral spinal fluid to the venous circulation.

[14] The falx cerebri is a midline dural partition that separates the left and right hemispheres of the brain.

teachers to the living. We each gave our bodies willingly to advance the cause of science and medicine for the wellbeing of all humanity."

"Wait! What?" Gavin, struggling to keep pace with Arden's brisk walk, could not process the information quickly enough. "I'm dead?" His eyes were as blank as a fresh canvas.

"As a doornail," Cameo chimed in as he strolled alongside.

"But if I am dead, how is it that I am talking, moving, and...."

"Silence!" Arden abruptly stopped and sternly looked Gavin square in the face. "Take a deep breath."

Gavin pursed his lips and expanded his chest to inhale a bolus of air. Somewhat dismayed, he felt no air enter or leave his oral cavity. His confusion deepened to sheer panic. Gavin palpated his neck beneath the angle of his jaw, frantically searching for a carotid pulse. His artery was as motionless as an empty water hose. His fingers moved to his wrist. No pulse. Out of desperation, he placed his entire hand over his chest, hoping to feel the throb of his own heart.

"You will feel no rhythm because it does not exist. Your heart no longer beats, and your lungs will never inflate again," Arden stated in the form of an unwavering fact. It was clear Arden was the alpha male of the group. His authoritative demeanor paired well with his desert-camouflaged army pants and dog tags around his neck.

Arden took Gavin by the arm and walked him to Nyla's mirror at a strolling pace. The mirror was positioned beneath a high bar in the place where a padded mat would typically lie. Nyla was a graceful and supple gymnast. Her upper arm strength and sheer athleticism allowed her to execute flawless dismounts, one of which Gavin observed upon approach at the climax of her well-rehearsed routine.

Gavin leaned over the edge of Nyla's platform and peered intently at his reflection. He did not fully realize he was looking at himself until his hand reached for his face. Gavin saw for the first time his own musculature. He, too, was unclad. A small silver retractor hung from his arm and caught reflections of light when he moved. The retractor with its comb-like teeth pushed aside his deltoid and bicep muscles to reveal metal hardware mending his broken shoulder. In the midline of his forehead, his frontal bone sat exposed from the separation of his frontalis muscles. Gavin stood frozen hunched over the mirror in silence as he processed his new physique.

"How did this happen? Where is my skin?" Gavin shuddered, not knowing which question to ask next.

"You did a number on your shoulder, but you must have had a superb surgeon. That is one of the cleanest repairs I've seen." Arden disregarded Gavin's questions and gestured to Cameo, "Look at this dissection! His suprascapular artery and nerve are pristine." Arden, a lieutenant in his own right, muttered, "The army goes over the bridge, the navy goes under." Though Galen did not understand the reference, he chose not to inquire further.

"As you become more comfortable with your new persona, you will better understand and appreciate this gift." Arden strained to express encouragement. "When we enter into the plastinate realm, we take on the new persona and name our creator has given us. For you, the creator has chosen the name Galen, which means *healer* in Greek. As such, you will learn to possess the knowledge and competence of a skilled physician." Despite Arden's congenial smile, Galen was reluctant to trust him. "Know that for every day that passes, you will remember less and less of your past life until the point when you will no longer remember who you once were."

With Arden's hand on Galen's shoulder, they turned and sat on Nyla's reflective surface. "How could I be a doctor?" Galen scoffed in amazement. "I don't even know where my thyroid is located…that's in your chest, right?" Arden grimaced.

"I get queasy at the sight of blood." Doubt pervaded Galen like spreading mold. "None of this can be real," he insisted, hoping to talk his way out of a worsening nightmare.

"Our blood has been drained," Arden reassured.

"My best friend, Morgan, wants to be a nurse, like her mother. She is great with blood, but not me. When her little brother gets hurt, she's the first to bandage him up. Whenever I see blood, I cover my eyes and try not to dry heave. I'm getting nauseous just thinking about it." Galen rubbed his abdomen and took in two deep air-less breaths to quell his queasy stomach.

"What is the last thing you remember?" Arden asked.

"I remember being helplessly paralyzed and covered with a cold, damp cloth," Galen reluctantly replied, trying to purge the image from his mind.

"No, before that," Arden pressed.

CHAPTER 4

THE CODE OF SILENCE

Galen stared into the distance as he strained to recall his last moments. "It was midday. I was with Morgan, a girl...," Galen deliberately slowed his speech to ensure enough space between words and to emphasize, "...*friend*. On our way home from watching her brother's little league baseball game, we stopped for our favorite treat, *Harold's Ice Cream*. I ordered a medium brownie delight topped with a scoop of vanilla and whipped cream. Morgan settled on a small turtle sundae. She's not had much of an appetite these days. I remember moving her long hair away from her ice cream. She hardly ever wears her hair up and she's not the best at being self-aware." Galen smiled at the fond daydream of Morgan and her quirks.

"You know, Morgan is even more competitive than I am. She loves sports. She always wanted to play softball, but her mother would never allow it." The excitement in Galen's voice quickly waned to a somber soliloquy. "When we were in primary school together, she was diagnosed with cardiomyopathy. Her heart has difficulty meeting the regular demands of her body, let alone exhaustive sports. She would give anything to be healthy and energetic like her brother, Spencer. Despite her medical problems, she always has a positive outlook on life. That's what I love about her the most. She makes everyone else's problems seem more important and bigger than her own. Of course, they never are."

Galen stood up from the platform and traipsed back and forth in front of Arden like a child waiting for a bus on the first day of school. His chin turned up at Arden as he spoke, "About a month ago, I learned the medications she was prescribed since her initial diagnosis were no longer working. What began as a minor controllable disease, has now progressed to a life-threatening illness." Galen's worry was as heavy as a wheelbarrow of wet clay. "Recently, Morgan's doctors added her to the heart transplant list. Without a donor's heart, she may not survive another year. When I found out, I felt so hopeless. Morgan is everything to me. Beneath the surface, I felt my heart rip in two. I would do anything to protect her, but now the fate of her life is beyond anything I can control."

In a fleeting moment of heartache, Galen swiftly brushed the corner of his eye to intercept an invisible tear. He was far too macho to publicly display his emotions. In school, the slightest slip of sensitivity would have landed him months of ridicule and heckling. The last thing he needed was to be branded as a *Sensitive Sophie* by a group of unfamiliar corpses. He inhaled a sharp sniff and stood tall.

"We were sitting curbside at one of the café's quaint rod iron tables. A blue and white striped vinyl umbrella propped at an angle shielded us from the sun and helped prolong the life of our ice cream. Morgan was teaching me how to make an origami swan from a paper napkin when her mom arrived to pick her up. I was planning to walk home. Before she left, Morgan gave me a fiendish smile, tagged me, and said, "Got ya last!" It's a perpetual game of tag we've played since primary school that never ends." Even without skin, Arden sensed Galen was blushing. "In the near distance, the sound of worn tires speeding over a cobblestone street caught my attention. An olive-colored sedan had gone rogue. It was out of control and headed straight for the café."

Remembering the last seconds before his demise, Galen exclaimed in astonishment, "No! It can't be!" The seriousness of the situation fully set in like a prison sentence. Terrified and stricken with agony, Galen asked, "Morgan… Where is she? Is she okay? I have to find her!"

Concerned but defensive, Arden interrupted, "You are irrational! While you may have feelings for this girl, to have the dead walk among the living would upset the order. Besides, if you did find her, the Code of Silence forbids you from speaking directly with the living."

"But you don't understand. Morgan is everything to me. I have to know that she's okay," Galen pleaded.

Arden, now standing firm like a colonel, sternly replied, "Galen, you still have much to learn about this new world. What you have yet to understand is that, as cadavers, we are the entrusted guardians of undiscovered medical knowledge. It is we who share and divulge life-changing scientific information at its appointed time." Arden raised his hand at Galen to thwart his pressing eagerness to interrupt. "If the release of essential knowledge occurs too early or is revealed to the wrong person, there could be dire consequences that could alter the existence of the human race. The Code of Silence is not only to protect the integrity of our kind but, more importantly, to protect the greater scientific wisdom entrusted to us. Any bequeathed body who violates this Code of Silence will die indefinitely."

"Aren't we already dead," Galen remarked snidely.

"Yes, we are dead," Arden answered. "Yet we are still under the supremacy of a higher intelligent power; a power so great that his unmatched authority is absolute. Whether man, woman, or child, any preserved flesh who breaks this code will return instantly to the dust from which they once came."

"If we are wardens of undiscovered medical knowledge, then is there a cure for Morgan's condition?" If Galen's mental gears were real, they would have been spinning fast enough to hear a hum.

Arden redirected. "As I said before, for every day that passes, you will not only forget who you once were, but will no longer remember your family, your friends, or what they meant to you."

"But you didn't answer my question. Is there a cure or not?" Galen pressed exuding more confrontational body language than he intended. He went with it and leaned in just like his debate coach had taught him.

Arden sighed like a parent giving into a child's temper tantrum. "Ribozore," he stated.

"Are you swearing at me?" asked Galen, his posture becoming more defensive.

Arden responded with a slight roll of his eyes. "New members of the plastinate realm don't typically learn this information on their first day." Feeling the need to busy himself, Arden swiped a cloth from a neighboring textile-themed platform and began dusting the exhibit. "I guess it wouldn't *kill* me to tell you now."

"Very punny!"

"As our resident physician, you would have learned about it eventually anyway." Arden straightened a few slanted books on the next platform. Cleaning was his mindless escape. "Ribozore is a potent synthetic drug in the early stages of clinical trials. Knowledge of this medication was recently released. Like seeds ready for nurturing, these morsels of planted knowledge will sprout and eventually bloom to save many lives." Galen listened carefully with skepticism, feeling the pedantic metaphor was overkill.

"Three years ago, Dr. Simon Floundary and his research team at Heidelberg University Hospital discovered Ribozore. One of Simon's graduate students was rotating through two different research labs. In Simon's lab, the student was studying the progression of genetic cardiomyopathy. In the other lab, he was studying the effects of novel drugs on the pancreas. In preparation for Simon's canine test subjects' weekly functional scans, the graduate student unknowingly mixed a vial of procedural contrast with a medication intended to alter the structural development of pancreatic cells. The heart scans were uninterpretable because of the error. However, within a week of the mishap, Simon noticed peculiar changes in the treatment group's behavior. Upon necropsy, the canine hearts were void of the characteristics common to genetic cardiomyopathy. From that point forward, Dr. Floundary began studying Ribozore as a treatment for cardiomyopathy in humans. A clinical trial of Ribozore is now underway to determine the best dosage for adults with the fewest side effects. Testing in teens and pediatric patients is unlikely to begin until at least phase three of the trial."

"Let me get this straight," Galen responded a little dazed by the information overload. "So, Morgan needs to begin a regimen of Ribozore because the medication will restructure the cellular architecture of her myocardium. It will reverse the effects of her obstructive hypertrophic cardiomyopathy." Galen paused, stunned at the words that spewed unconsciously from his mouth. Never had he spoken with such certitude. Even Arden was impressed with his fluent medical jargon. "Ribozore will practically cure her and allow her to live a normal life?"

"I see your new persona is already taking hold." Arden was proud to see Galen acclimating to his new fund of knowledge quicker than most.

"My old self would have never said that! How, all of a sudden, do I know anything about medicine?" Galen's first taste of his new abilities put him into a frenzy.

Arden grinned with delight. "Watching new cadavers mature into their personas is always so rewarding."

"But I feel like an imposter, a fraud."

"You'll settle into your new identity the more you learn about it. You're already more competent in your new persona than you realize." Arden had a real knack for judiciously explaining complex information. "You see, as cadavers, we gain knowledge exponentially in our areas of concentration. How we learn is analogous to machine learning." Arden, now at his own platform, rummaged through an old army trunk surrounded by other military paraphernalia. "Where is that blasted notebook?" Like pulling a bowling ball from a helmet, Arden withdrew an excessively thick rolled-up handbook from a hollowed-out missile shell adjacent to the trunk. "Here we are!" he exclaimed.

"Just like machine learning, there are two types of learning we experience, but to a higher degree." Much to Galen's dismay, lecturing seemed to come naturally to Arden. "First, there is supervised learning. That's what this handbook is for." Arden plopped the textbook-sized manual into Galen's hands. It looked like it was from the 12th century. "And, secondly, there is unsupervised learning. It is this latter form of learning that gives you the metaphysical ability to identify hidden patterns and intrinsic nuances of data, factoids, and useless information." Arden's expressiveness was nauseating. "Furthermore, our working and long-term memories have the same capacity allowing us to store, manipulate, and extrapolate information in ways that are incomprehensible to the living." Arden's passionate gesturing confirmed how proud he was of whom he had become.

Galen, on the other hand, felt like a pledge being sworn into a secret society he had no desire to be a part of. While joining a college fraternity was once a tempting thought, in the here and now, the idea lost its appeal. Reality crept in with a vengeance as Galen's craving to return to his old life uncontrollably grew more distant. Thinking of Morgan was the simplest distraction for ignoring actuality.

"Given Morgan's prognosis, she needs this medication now. She could die within a year or even sooner. There's no time to wait for more testing." Galen flipped through the dense manual one page at a time starting randomly near the center. "How are these anatomy plates and physiology diagrams supposed to help me? What I need is a way to get Ribozore to Morgan."

Arden interjected before Galen could utter another thought, "That's not possible."

"As a physician, isn't it my responsibility to alleviate pain and suffering and restore health in all patients?" Galen argued. "Didn't Plato or Aristotle or some old dead dude say that?"

"Your immediate responsibility is to learn your new persona. And what you just recited is the spirit of the Hippocratic Oath, penned by none other than the distinguished Greek physician Hippocrates."

"Won't Dr. Floundary eventually learn that Ribozore is safe and most effective in younger patients? If we have this knowledge, then why can't I save her now?" Galen huffed a deliberate breath, despite his non-compliant lungs being incapable of gas exchange. "Why can't I share what I know to not only save her but hundreds of other innocent people who suffer from the same condition?" Galen disputed Arden's position with unbridled concern. "I can't stand idly by. I have to save Morgan. I must, at least, try. I'll do whatever it takes. Even if it means giving up whatever life I have left." Galen skated away from Arden in frustration as he strained to formulate a feasible plan.

Arden pursued him and rebutted, "I understand you are upset and concerned about your high school sweetheart, but it is not worth the risk."

"She is not my girlfriend!"

"Sure kid. You're just head over heels for her and regret not telling her how you felt before you died."

"Keep it above the belt. That was a low blow," Galen retorted.

"The quicker you accept the truth and your new reality, the better you'll feel. Besides, it is true, isn't it?"

"I'll neither confirm nor deny." Galen crossed his arms as he turned his back to Arden wishing he had a private room with a door he could slam.

"That's a yes." Arden jabbed. "If you try to save Morgan, you could expose our kind, placing all of us in jeopardy. Releasing knowledge before its appointed time can have causal effects beyond our comprehension."

"But it's the right thing to do!" Galen exclaimed as he threw the manual to the floor releasing his raw frustration.

"Right, in whose eyes?" There was no stopping the argument now. "You cannot let your newly attained knowledge cloud your judgment. Besides, you would compromise the work of the medical school cadavers. It is their duty to regulate scientific knowledge at their respective academic institutions. Cadavers in the armed forces test the effects of munitions on the human body. They manage military intelligence and the release of new weapons for biowarfare." Arden's irate rant was both demoralizing and impressive. "Cadavers who are crash test subjects oversee safety developments and the use of new technologies for preventing automobile accidents. All cadavers have an assigned responsibility only to bestow knowledge at the appointed time. As plastinated beings, we are obligated to educate the next generation and instill a predilection for medicine within them. You have not been delegated to release this intimate knowledge of Ribozore to Dr. Simon Floundary. You must stand down soldier before you unbalance the order of biomedical knowledge."

Suddenly, a flood of light entered through the glass rimming the upper east wall. It illuminated the entire rotunda. The breaking of dawn signaled the return of the employees. Like clockwork, employees would soon arrive at the museum in preparation for the day's events. In the coming hours, droves of onlookers would

meander through the popular Plastination Planet exhibit, eagerly pointing, grimacing, and staring in awe.
Knowing what was to come, Arden escorted Galen to
his platform. A display case full of early 20th-century
medical instruments accentuated the staging. Handing
Galen an x-ray of a humeral neck fracture, Arden lifted
Galen's right arm to portray him as an inquisitive physician reviewing a film by the ceiling's light.

After all he had encountered on his first night, Galen
had yet one last thing to learn. Arden, as the watchman
and leader of the plastinated cadavers, determined
when the plastinates would solidify. At the word *moritati*, Latin for *play dead*, all cadaveric motion ceased ren-
dering each cadaver fixed in whatever posture they assumed.

"Tomorrow, I will introduce you to the rest of your
companions. After a full day of fixation, you'll be renewed and will have a better appreciation for what you
have learned about our kind." Arden explained in haste
as he tidied up around his podium. "Per the code of qui-
escence, we must remain dormant from sunrise to sun-
set."

"Is there a code of boredom, too?" Galen asked facetiously. "With so many rules, how can anybody have
fun around here?"

"Are you ready?" Arden questioned choosing to ignore the neophyte's comment.

Adjacent to Galen's platform, Arden slowly stepped
up onto his display adorned with military regalia. Once
standing squarely behind the old trunk covered by a

decorated lieutenant's uniform, Arden carefully set himself in a heroic stance. Raising his right hand to his brow with his palm pronated, Arden assumed a salute and sounded a warning, "Take your places!" and then, "Moritati!"

CHAPTER 5

EVERY BODY

The custodian flipped off the showroom spotlights at the subpanel one section at a time. The museum's required safety lighting gave a dusky glow at the periphery of the rotunda. Seconds after the lights dimmed, loose keys chattered as the guard locked the exhibit doors one by one. The exhibit was secure. No one was getting in.

Arden was the first to awake, and after a drawn-out yawn, he bellowed, "Excito sursum!" Every plastinated cadaver came to life from their slumber.

Galen, a tad sluggish, stretched his arms. For a moment, he took in the wonderment of the spectacle and watched the early evening rituals of several cadavers. One female body, whose platform portrayed a florist's shop consumed by arrangements of faux flowers, swept around her display to tidy up after the day's visitors. Another body, wearing a leather apron a few feet away, meticulously rearranged fake fruits and vegetables displayed like a produce stand at a farmer's market. A third body with her hair tied up in a ponytail strolled past carrying a small stack of books as if heading to a café for leisurely reading. The entire backdrop and milieu resembled a scene taken straight from a computer-animated film. Anxious to meet every body, Galen turned toward Arden's display only to find him absent. Between the two platforms, Cassius stared up at Galen from the floor.

Cassius was the first to speak, "I'm sorry if I startled you yesterday when you awoke. We usually have Cameo meet the new bodies, with his skin on, of course. Although he's nude, it's not nearly as awkward to meet him as it is to encounter the rest of us."

"That…makes sense," Galen concurred not knowing what else to say.

"Arden is tending to some business. He asked that I show you around. Do you mind?"

"Not at all."

"Great, come with me. We have much to see." Cassius extended his hand to help Galen from his platform.

Cassius was a short, stout man. He wore black thick-rimmed glasses and appeared to be of Chinese descent, though without knowing his exact skin tone and features it was difficult to be certain. He was effectively a walking, talking human chest of drawers. Instead of finding garments tucked neatly within each drawer, there were organs arranged like three-dimensional puzzle pieces. All that was missing to complete the full effect were brass knobs. As a consequence of his disposition, Cassius walked with an awkward, uncoordinated gait. With each forward and backward movement in the sagittal plane, his drawers clacked as they slid open and closed. His subtle compensatory waddle from side to side only partly subdued his loose visceral coffers.

It was evident Cassius was on a mission. If he timed it right, Galen could meet every cadaver in the exhibit and take a tour of the museum within the six hours they had before resuming their moritati poses. Galen, on the other hand, was in no hurry and was easily distracted by the cackles coming from the poker table in the corner.

"Who are they?" Galen questioned.

"That is Otto and Otis," Cassius politely responded. "And the poor soul they are making fun of is Ivan, Ivory's twin. Ivan is always the butt, or lack thereof, of their jokes. He can't help but rattle when he walks. You should see him dance. He has plenty of rhythm."

Ivan, like Ivory, was a skeleton, though the color of his bones was not as pristine. His style was plain and modest, with only a black beret donning his head. Otis, overhearing Cassius, seized the opportunity to give Galen a demonstration. "Hey Ivan, what's your favorite meal?" Before Ivan had a chance to speak, Otis interrupted, "Wait, let me guess, spareribs!" Otis and Otto exchanged a moment of laughter until Otis came up with his next punchline. "Come on. Give me a smile." With no muscles for facial expressions, all Ivan could manage was to prop open his lower jaw for a smile. "Yes. I agree. Our humor is jaw-dropping." Otis couldn't resist. He broke out in a rage of searing laughter all over again.

"He's just getting warmed up," Cassius said. "Every

night, there are new insults and new jokes at Ivan's expense."

"Can't we just play poker?" Ivan urged.

"Ivan is not the best poker player. Let's just say he's very transparent," Cassius remarked as he made a nod to the full-length mirror propped behind Ivan. Through Ivan's intercostal spaces, his poker hand was in plain view of the hecklers.

"Ivan, I'd buy you a drink, but you'd need a mop as a chaser." Otto bantered.

Cassius rolled his eyes at the mockery and prodded Galen along. A gentleman at the next display over was deep in thought, playing chess against himself. "Allow me to introduce you to our astute chess aficionado and strategist, Cato." Cato, like the others, was skinless and magnificently dissected. His brain was exposed showing its vibrant arterial supply. His brachial plexus[15] was delicately displayed as the nerves running from his lower neck pierced the musculature of his arm and forearm.

"It is a pleasure to make your acquaintance. You must be Galen, our newest member," said Cato.

"I am. Do you not have a worthy opponent?"

In the voice of a Renaissance poet, Cato facetiously quoted, "What a piece of work is a man, how noble in reason, how infinite in faculties." Changing his tenor to his regular voice, he continued, "I am afraid I have no

---

[15] The brachial plexus is a network of nerves originating mostly from the cervical spinal cord. This nerve plexus innervates the muscles that act on the upper limb and carries sensory information from the upper limb back to the central nervous system.

one to challenge me. While our intellect is bountiful, no one here is interested in exercising critical thinking. Many are content with performing other, less mindful tasks."

Without warning, Vitalis appeared bright-eyed and bushy-tailed and whispered something into Cassius's ear. Then he darted away, exclaiming, "It's time…it's time!"

"That's too bad," Galen sympathized. "I wouldn't mind a friendly game or two."

"Really?" Cato seemed surprised.

"It will have to wait," Cassius butted in, "You, Galen, have a more pressing issue to tend to."

"I look forward to your company," Cato remarked.

Cassius prodded Galen along in the direction of a small crowd gathering at the other end of the exhibit hall. From behind them, Galen heard the obscured sounds of a horse's canter and slowed his pace. Before he could turn to inspect the commotion, a puff of cold air ran up his trapezius muscle, sending chills down his spine. An about-face landed Galen's wide eyes directly into the dark, gaping nostrils of a red beast. Not knowing whether to run or make himself as large and threatening as possible, he slowly backed away from the docile creature. When the entire animal came into view, a body could be seen perched on top.

"Welcome to the Plastination Planet exhibit. I'm Philip," said the man atop the creature. "Hippos, my trusty steed, recognizes bodies by their scent. You must be new. Otherwise, he would not have stopped to introduce himself."

Hippos, now satisfied with Galen's scent, grew restless and began side-stepping against Philip's wishes.

"I'm Galen."

"You're Galen? Perfect, you are just the body I was looking for. I am headed to Juno now. Hop on. I'll take you there."

Hearing the urgency in his tone, Galen did not question Philip's intentions. He mounted Hippos with a blundering shove from Cassius. Before Galen had settled himself atop the muscular stallion, they were off trotting toward the end of the exhibit hall.

"Where are we going?" shouted Galen over the clatter of horse hooves against the hard marble floor.

"Juno is giving birth! She needs a doctor."

"How will I help you find a doctor? I barely know anyone."

"You are the doctor!" Philip's crooked grin was just out of Galen's view.

Just as the realization set in, they arrived at Juno's feet. She was lying in the lithotomy position. Galen, with Philip's help, dismounted Hippos in a less than graceful manner. Arden's familiar face stood at Juno's side. He held her hand to comfort her.

"Hello, ma'am." Galen's voice cracked like the squeak of a reed instrument. He had never seen a female's fully naked perineum before. It's not exactly what he expected. Then again, everything looks different without skin.

Juno looked just like any other woman in labor, except her womb was exposed. It reminded Galen of lifting the side panel of an antique car's hood to see the engine. Except, instead of a greasy engine, there was a restless fetus curled into a tiny ball occasionally poking his palm into his mother's side.

Without thinking, Galen blurted, "How is that basketball supposed to fit through the net?"

"We'll work on your bedside manner," Arden said as he pulled Galen to the side.

"I'm sorry, but I don't think I can help. I have never assisted in a medical emergency before." Galen stammered, overwhelmed with nervousness.

"Calm yourself. You have the knowledge of a great physician." Arden looked from side to side around Galen. "Where is your handbook?"

"Here it is, sir!" barked a winded Cassius who had run to retrieve it knowing Arden's intent.

Without hesitation, Arden flipped directly to a reference image of the perineum. "Study this image." Arden momentarily returned to Juno's side to comfort her as her feigned Lamaze breaths quickened. "Now, focus your thoughts. Allow your new persona to take control."

"I've had thirty seconds to study one page. I can't even pronounce the names of half of these structures. This is like giving a toddler scissors to cut your hair.

You're insane if you expect me to deliver a baby!"

"We also have photographic memories. You just need to glance at the page to retain the information. You'll be fine." Arden put his hands on Galen's shoulders and whispered into his ear, "It's time. Relax. Think happy thoughts. Better yet, think of Morgan."

"As a naked woman in labor?" Galen shrieked in an insecure tone.

"No," Arden responded. "Think of Morgan as a supportive friend who encourages you to face your fears and to realize your full potential."

Galen closed his eyes and took a deep airless breath. He held out his arms in a meditative posture as if trying to summon his new persona.

"What is he doing?" Cassius whispered to Arden. Arden shrugged.

"I need to see if the baby is crowning," Galen said with only modest confidence. In viewing the exposed fetus, he realized the baby was breech. Its head, positioned superiorly, touched the uterine fundus. The child's feet, nestled near the cervix, pressed against Juno's urinary bladder. "Juno, we will need to deliver the baby via cesarean section," Galen said more calmly as his persona began to take over. He cautiously scooped his hands around the fetus through the womb's preexisting aperture left by the creator's dissection. With the newborn safely cradled in his hands, he delivered the child from his mother. Galen instructed a bystander, whom he had not yet met, to clamp the umbilical cord with the Kelly clamps Arden had waiting. The bystander followed his orders and without further instruction, divided the umbilical cord with one swift slice of his hand.

Galen placed the whaling child in his mother's arms. The tranquility of Juno's endearing cuddle immediately soothed him. Juno hugged Galen with her free hand. "Thank you for delivering my son."

Galen was visibly relieved to have the experience behind him. "What's his name?"

"Cletus," Juno replied.

Galen respectfully nodded in agreement. "Cletus the fetus. It suits him. I wish you a speedy recovery."

The crowd around Juno had already dissipated. Excusing himself from Juno's side, Galen approached his surgical assistant to thank him for his services. No longer caught up in the moment, Galen took a closer look at his tall and unsteady helper.

CHAPTER 6

COUNTING THE DAYS

Galen's hand clutched that of a man who resembled a loaf of sandwich bread sliced horizontally from head to toe. "To whom do I owe the pleasure?"

"I'm Tome." Each of his slices had the same thickness and rigidity as ten-gauge sheet metal. "But if you ever run into one of my sections, they are named according to their serial numbers." He was referring to a single slice of his body.

"Convenient. I'll keep that in mind," Galen acknowledged. "Is there a local watering hole nearby?" The large showroom with its copious isles of furbished displays was difficult to navigate. "I'd like to buy you a soda to properly thank you. Given my hands won't stop shaking, I need some caffeine to calm my nerves."

"Next door is a locomotive exhibit with a dining car. Except drinks aren't my thing. Drinks run through me like water runs through a sieve. No one likes to drink standing in a wet puddle. I learned that lesson the hard way." The topic was a particularly sore spot for Tome. "The dining car is this way."

Galen followed Tome toward a pillar-lined archway

dividing the two showrooms. Cassius, waddling like a duck, followed suit. As they approached the entrance of the neighboring industrial era exhibit, Galen found himself fixated on the most peculiar oddity. Before Galen could rationalize his bewilderment, Cassius interjected.

"Vitalis is obsessed with training it how to leap over benches. He also thinks he'll be able to ride it soon."

To the side of the hall, away from the thoroughfare of active bodies, Vitalis held a lead line that encircled the beak and neck of a gangly salmon-colored ostrich. Its dark charcoal-stained feathers were immaculately preserved on its wings and tail while the rest of the bird was exposed. Running along the length of the ostrich's neck were delicate, paper-thin muscles. Galen admired the lattice-like muscular pattern that complimented the bird's elongated pearly white trachea and blush-toned esophagus. The ostrich dropped a long slender object at Vitalis's feet and shuffled backward in excitement, waiting for Vitalis's command.

"You can't keep taking Ivan's fibula!"[16] Vitalis scolded his avian friend. He patted the ostrich on the head and flung the ossified object straight up into the air. The flightless bird caught it before it hit the marble floor.

Just beyond Vitalis's training grounds, Galen's eyes trailed off to a black box hanging on the wall. He took two steps forward. "Is that a working phone?" Galen

---

[16] The leg, between the knee and ankle joint, is made of two bones. The larger weight-bearing shinbone is the tibia. The thinner outer bone that parallels the tibia is called the fibula. The distal end of the fibula flares to form the lateral malleolus; the prominent bump felt on the outer ankle.

asked Cassius.

"Sure is," Cassius replied. Galen abandoned the group before Cassius could finish his thought. Realizing Galen's intentions, Cassius gave chase with an uncoordinated trot hoping to subdue his rattling drawers. "We can't speak to the living. Remember the Code of Silence!" Cassius shouted over the social hum of the other bodies, but it was no use. Galen's youthful inquisitiveness and spontaneous escape were no match for Cassius.

Galen, operating on pure emotion, grabbed the receiver. He feverishly dialed Morgan's cell phone. With each ring, Galen's disappointment grew. "Please answer, please answer," he pleaded under his breath. He had to know that she was safe.

"Thanks for calling Bickers and Bickers divorce attorneys at law. How may I assist you with your marital needs?" Galen hung up the receiver and dialed again, the correct number this time.

Another three rings went unanswered. Assuming the worst, Galen slowly lowered the phone from his ear. "Hello," answered a tender voice on the other end. He snapped the phone back to his ear. "Hello," said Morgan. Galen, speechless, fell weak in the knees. He listened intently and tightened every muscle in his body to contain his urge to respond. He recognized the rhythmic beep of an EKG in the background. The urge to respond grew even stronger. As he pursed his lips to utter her name, a shrilling screech blared behind him. Galen impulsively slammed the phone against the receiver, fearful he had made a grave mistake. Vitalis aggressively yanked the lead line of the boisterous and uncooperative ostrich.

Realizing the emotional weight of the moment, Cassius gently prodded. "Was that Morgan?" he somberly asked. "Arden mentioned her before you awoke."

"Yes, and I know where she is." Galen's optimism faded. He realized he may never speak to her again.

"During the exhibition, we all become restless at times," Tome said, reacting to Vitalis's bold techniques, oblivious to the heart-to-heart exchange. "Training the ostrich seems to keep Vitalis busy. Frankly, it keeps him from being underfoot if you know what I mean. Before the ostrich arrived, Vitalis would polish everyone's stage each night. I'm not a clinician, but I think Vitalis has a touch of OCD," Tome speculated.

"What do you mean, 'during exhibition'?" Galen inquired as the three strolled to the dining car.

Tome quickly fielded the question with more eagerness than Galen was prepared for. "Our exhibit shows around the world! Every eight months, we are crated and shipped to another museum to be put on display. They market our exhibit as 'An unforgettable journey into the human body.' We teach the living what it means to be human and inspire the next generation of medical professionals and scientists." Tome's enthusiasm was contagious.

"How long have you been in this location on exhibit?" Galen pressed.

"It's hard to say," replied Cassius. "Most of us find it hard to keep track of time. A typical byproduct of death, I suppose. Cato might know. He likes to keep a journal."

As Cassius finished his thought, both Cato and Marcel came into view in the dining car. On approach, the magnitude of the train car caught Galen by surprise. Even though the hunter-green railcar had ended its service on the Imperial Railways in 1890, its original beauty and grandeur were undisturbed. The only modification was a missing external wall for better public viewing of the car from ground level.

Cassius motioned to Cato and Marcel. As the trio climbed the metal grates of the car's tarnished stairs, Cato and Marcel made room for their onboarding.

"Welcome to the *Covered Hopper*, where the hops are as stiff and cold as the patrons," said Marcel as he greeted Galen for the first time since his awakening.

"Great! I'll have a soda," said Galen.

"Come on kid. Live a little." Marcel amused the rest of the group at Galen's expense. "Are you afraid your mom will kill you for sipping the vine's nectar? News flash! You're already dead."

Galen played along. He was anxious to relax and wanted to fit in. He guzzled half a pint of brew. As he lowered the mug, disgust caused his *Elvis* muscle[17] to curl his upper lip. "What is that?"

"It's not the drink," remarked Cato. "It's you. You're

---

[17] The anatomical name for the *Elvis* muscle is the levator labii superioris alaeque nasi muscle; the longest named muscle in the human body. This muscle curls the upper lip while simultaneously flaring the nostril.

tasting formalin from the fixation process. You'll get used to it after a while. If you start with a shot of InfuTrace, it's more tolerable."

"Wow! If I weren't already dead, I would think you were trying to poison me," Galen joked trying to fit in.

"This world has much to offer, but it comes with a price," remarked Cato.

"Like losing the memories of your past," Galen reflected.

"True."

"How much longer do I have before I forget my past life?"

"I'm an avid journaler," said Cato. "When I first arrived, I penned every fond memory I could think of and scribed every detail of my new experience. The first memories to fade were the names of my loved ones. Within six days of arriving, the ink holding the memories of my past disappeared. All that remained were the entries of my new life."

"How long was I here before I awoke?"

"Newbies usually spend two days in the prep room before going on display," returned Cato.

Counting the days, Galen pondered aloud, "So, I only have four days to save Morgan?"

"Save Morgan?" Cassius exclaimed. "You can't be serious!"

"Who's Morgan?" Marcel butted in.

"It's hard to explain," replied Galen.

Cassius, the softy of the group, thought otherwise. "Morgan is Galen's Juliet who is dying of a genetic heart disease unless he can find some way to give her a new synthetic drug that will save her life! It's all very romantic."

Galen winced at the thought of what else Cassius might know about the intimate details of his personal life. "Thank you, Cassius. I'll take it from here."

"I must do something. We grew up together, and she's my best friend. She deserves a normal life," Galen urged.

"Correction," Cato interrupted, staring down at one of his journal entries. "Technically, you have only three days to save Morgan. At dawn, in three days, we'll be packed into crates in preparation for transport. Once sealed, we're encased in darkness until we arrive at our new location."

Under the table, Tome's knees jittered vigorously. His sections slid out of alignment from his core like a loose deck of playing cards. "Arden will not allow this. I assure you, he will not," blurted Tome.

"Don't you remember what it felt like to lose your past life?" interjected Cato. "It's so bleak and lonely. If we have a chance to help Galen fulfill his final wish, then we should help him. We're here to strengthen solidarity and to leave a mark on the world we left behind." With fortitude, Cato slammed his hand onto the center of the table. "I'm in! Who's with me?"

"I don't know, Cato," Cassius whined. "Tome's point

is valid. We all know Arden will not support this. Plus, there is no way to ensure our safety out in the real world. One slip-up and the code could take us, just like that!" Cassius snapped his finger for added effect.

"Where's your sense of adventure?" Marcel chimed in as his thick hand clobbered Cato's. "Come on. The danger can't be any worse than sneaking Long Johns from Mr. Camper's bakery." Marcel looked straight at Cassius. "That's right...I know you stuff your drawers." Cassius recoiled in his seat.

Marcel, seeing mostly an opportunity for adventure, leaned into Cato's argument, "We need to make the most of our gifts in this life. We need to pay it forward through action, not inaction. We stand dormant on display day in and day out, passively hoping to ignite a passion for anatomy in anyone who passes by. Now, we have a chance to save a life! This is a once-in-a...second-lifetime opportunity!"

Surprisingly, Marcel's words struck a chord with Cassius, the least likely of the bunch to approve. Cassius pledged his allegiance to the cause by placing his hand on top of the others. Marcel jabbed his rigid elbow into Tome's gut. After re-adjusting his midsection, Tome also complied by piling his hand slices on top like poker chips.

"Well, Galen, what do you say? Are you ready to save your Juliet?"

With a look of determination, Galen rested his skinless hand on Tome's sections, "I'm all in. Whatever it takes."

"Then it's settled," Cato affirmed. "Tomorrow night, we'll devise a plan at the jazz club."

CHAPTER 7

DIAMOND IN THE ROUGH

Mina Lowe sat quietly in a dull yellow leather chair in the corner of a quaint hospital room. Her crossed legs held an open undisturbed novel in her lap. A windowpane fogged with condensation blurred her fixed gaze on a distant streetlamp.

"Mom," Morgan called, rousing Mina from her daze. "You haven't read a single page in over five minutes. What are you staring at?"

"Nothing, sweetheart." Mina straightened her posture, incapable of concealing her tired fretful eyes. "I'm sorry. I'm not myself these days. Do you need another pillow or blanket? Are you comfortable?"

"Mom, I'm fine. It's you I'm worried about."

Mina drifted to the edge of Morgan's bed. Morgan repositioned the bundle of EKG leads so her mother could nestle up close on the bed. Morgan's breathing was shallow. Her face was pale, and her hands were clammy.

"Don't worry about me, little one. Save your strength. You'll need it for when you get home. When I spoke with your grandmother, she said your brother misses you dearly, and he can't wait until you're home." Mina intertwined her fingers with Morgan's free hand. "I understand Spencer has learned a new magic trick. He's sure you'll be amazed. Even if you're not amazed, you know the routine." Mina smirked at Morgan with raised eyebrows. "He looks up to you, you know."

As Morgan exchanged a congenial grin with her mother, her sparkling pink cell phone chimed next to her on the bed sheet. The number was unfamiliar. Uncertain of whether to answer, Morgan waited three rings and then responded with a tender, "Hello."

No reply. Morgan listened intently but heard only the murmur of muffled voices masked by the buzz of an old static landline.

"Hello," Morgan said again, this time a touch louder than the first.

Morgan pressed the phone tightly to her ear to decipher the perplexing background noise. Unexpectedly, a loud, piercing squawk of a bird nearly ruptured her ear drum. The line went dead.

"Who was that?" Morgan's mother inquired, hearing the obscure noise herself.

"That was bizarre. It must have been a pocket dial from someone walking through a zoo."

"A zoo?" Mina questioned as if she had misheard her daughter. "At this late hour? That is strange. Perhaps someone was watching an animal documentary," Mina rationalized.

"Tomorrow is an important day. We'll find out from

the doctors if you're ready to go home. Let's turn in for the night," Mina urged her daughter.

"I miss him," Morgan said softly, trying to disguise her emotions. Morgan looked down and adjusted the silver charm bracelet around her wrist. She gently clinched one of the charms, a modest rough blue diamond suspended from a bail pendant, as if giving her departed friend a heartfelt hug. Gavin had given her the charm on her sixteenth birthday. It took him 10 months to save enough money from odd jobs just to afford a 0.15-carat gem in the rough. "He always said I was a diamond in the rough," Morgan recalled as she fought to hold back tears. Ever since they were teenagers, Gavin called her a diamond in the rough, mostly because of her athletic potential her parents would never allow her to pursue. When Morgan's parents were not around, Morgan and Gavin would sneak in some long toss or hit up the batting cages. So long as the activity did not involve running, Morgan was just as good at it, if not better than Gavin. Gavin was Morgan's escape from the impenetrable bubble her parents had erected around her.

"Gavin cared a lot about you. Never forget that," Mina stated. "He said you were the strongest person he knew." Mina, as a nurse, had the genuine gift of consolement. "I know you miss him. We all do. Part of me wishes he would walk straight through that door at any moment, but unfortunately, he won't. There is a time for mourning and a time for laughter. Grieving is perfectly natural," Mina reassured. "You can always keep him right here." She tapped Morgan's chest pointing to her heart. Having watched Gavin and Morgan grow up together, Mina knew their relationship had started to bloom differently right before Gavin's passing. After all the time they had spent together over the years, Gavin had become an extended part of their family. Mina missed him dearly too.

Mina tucked the covers snuggly under Morgan's chin, gave her a delicate kiss on the cheek, and reached behind her hospital bed to dim the lights. She returned to the ugly yellow leather chair, covered her legs with an extra hospital blanket, and reclined to get as comfortable as the chair would allow. Mina's warm motherly voice washed over Morgan from across the room, "Good night, honey."

Not long after dawn, a firm rapping at the door woke both Mina and Morgan.

"Come in," Mina reflexively called, running her fingers through her hair to make herself presentable.

"Hello, and good morning," announced an unrecognizable visitor. A slender fellow of average height emerged from the shadows of the doorway. He wore a white lab coat over top of a maroon and white checkered shirt. His hair was dark and curly. Speckles of silver peppered his sideburns.

Unlike others who had frequented Morgan's room, the collar of his white coat lacked a stethoscope. The cursive navy-blue script over his coat's pocket ended with a Ph.D. instead of the customary M.D. Trained as a translational researcher, Dr. Simon Floundary spent most of his time processing tissue samples and trialing the effects of new drug therapies using animal models in a laboratory setting. While his credentials allowed him to administer trial medications to lab animals, he required a collaborator with a medical license to conduct human subjects research. His role in overseeing the clinical drug trial required him to visit patients to monitor their medication compliance and health outcomes. Though, Simon would have much preferred to remain in the company of his animals.

"I don't think we've met before," said Mina.

"We've not yet had the pleasure. I'm Dr. Simon Floundary. It's very nice to meet you." The slight quiver of his vocal cords revealed his shy demeanor. "And you must be Morgan," Simon continued with an extended forearm reaching to shake Morgan's petite hand.

Groggy, Morgan rubbed her eyes and sluggishly uttered, "Good morning, did you bring breakfast?"

"Morgan!" Mina scolded her daughter in embarrassment.

"I'm afraid not," chuckled Dr. Floundary, "but I'll remember that for next time."

Simon turned his attention to Mina. "Mrs. Lowe, I work with Morgan's primary cardiologist, Dr. Ziegler. I have carefully read through Morgan's case file, and I think she is a prime candidate for a drug trial that I'm overseeing. I found Morgan's case to be particularly touching and familiar. I know what it's like to have a child in and out of the hospital. My 15-year-old son, Jesse, was recently diagnosed with a brain tumor. He'll be having surgery in the next few days to remove a mass that is pressing on his brainstem. As a parent, I know what it's like to be in your position. I wish I could switch places with my son. I wish there were something more I could do aside from holding his hand until he falls asleep at night. While my son's condition is precarious, I'm hopeful the progression of your daughter's condition will be very different."

"What do you mean?" Mina asked with a glimmer of hope.

"My research laboratory has been working on a new medication for cardiomyopathy. Currently, the drug is ending the second phase of a clinical trial that has focused on adult subjects. We hope to enter phase three of the trial next month where we will include teens and younger pediatric patients. We are preparing all the paperwork now before the next phase begins. I'm in the process of recruiting patients for this double-blind study. Given Morgan's case history, I feel she is a strong candidate for the trial."

"What do you mean by a double-blinded study?" inquired Morgan.

"We are testing the effectiveness of the trial drug compared to standard treatments. In a double-blind clinical trial, the medication the patient receives is unknown to both the patient and the research team until the trial is completed. As a study subject, neither you nor your mother will know if you have received the real medication or a placebo, effectively a sugar pill."

Dr. Floundary turned back to address Mina. "In Morgan's case, we would like to keep her on her current drug regimen throughout the trial, even though she is no longer responding to her medications. Keeping her therapy consistent will help us to determine how the new medication interacts in combination with other medications. This assumes she receives the active form of the medication and not the placebo, of course."

"Who decides if I receive the real medication or not," Morgan pressed.

"No one decides," Dr. Floundary explained. "A database houses the names of all study participants, and a computer algorithm decides at random who receives a placebo and who receives the trial medication."

"So you mean there is a 50% chance that Morgan could receive a sugar pill?" asked Mina, seeking clarification.

"That's correct," replied Dr. Floundary.

"You are telling me you want to give my daughter the only hope she has had for months, only to shatter her dream of a normal life when she learns she was part of a control group? Where will you be when I have to tell her she only has a few more months to live because a computer algorithm did not select her for the medication? I refuse to give my daughter false hope. I'm very sorry, Dr. Floundary, but Morgan will not be participating in the trial."

"I wanna do it!" shouted Morgan with unwavering

certainty.

"Morgan, as a minor, this is not your decision," her mother retorted.

"If Dad were here, he would agree with me, and you know it," countered Morgan with a flare of sass.

"I understand your concern, Mrs. Lowe." Dr. Simon Floundary inserted himself as he gauged the rising tension. "But this may be Morgan's only opportunity to receive the trial medication. Otherwise, she may have to wait until the drug reaches the market in another year or two. I do hope you'll give this serious consideration. Perhaps you would like to discuss this with your husband?"

"That's simply not possible," Mina sternly whispered as she brushed a tear from her cheek.

"He's dead!" Morgan blurted aloud. "A factory accident, three years ago."

"I am so sorry for your loss," Simon compassionately responded.

"If she joins the clinical trial, will she lose her place on the transplant list?" asked Mina with concern.

"If she joins the clinical trial, her position on the list will lower," answered Simon. "This is not a decision to take lightly. Would it be all right if I left some information with you?"

Mina nodded as if she had no other choice and reached to receive a colorful folder of Dr. Floundary's informational materials.

"It was a pleasure to meet you both."

As Dr. Floundary opened the door to leave, a familiar personality called out, "I brought breakfast!" Morgan immediately recognized her bestie, Paige. A prim and polished young lady, with her hair tied back in a ponytail, brushed past Dr. Floundary as she entered the room with a bright smile and unfiltered excitement.

"Is that what I think it is?" Morgan asked as she stared at the small brown paper sack dangling from Paige's fingers.

"It sure is!"

"Finally, some real food!" Morgan exclaimed as she unwrapped her favorite breakfast item, a salted bagel with strawberry cream cheese.

Mina acknowledged Paige with a smile, "Thank you for coming. It means a lot to Morgan."

"Now that you have company, I'm going to slip out to grab a coffee." Mina felt a bit selfish for wanting some alone time, but knew with Morgan being preoccupied, now was her best chance to sneak away for some solitude.

"Take your time, Mrs. Lowe," said Paige. "It's beautiful outside. Why don't you get some fresh air?"

"Thank you. I will," replied Mina with a look of appreciation.

Mina grabbed her satchel from the wooden cabinet opposite Morgan's bed. She left the room en route to a quaint coffee shop kitty-corner from the hospital grounds. As she waited for the elevator, with her mind in a fog, Morgan's lead cardiologist, Dr. Ziegler, called out from across the corridor, "Mrs. Lowe, Do you have a moment?"

"Of course, doctor. How are you this morning?" Mina responded as politely as her exhaustion would allow.

"I'm fine, thank you," Dr. Ziegler acknowledged. "I was hoping to discuss your daughter's condition with you." The doctor took Mina by the elbow and led her to a quiet waiting room only a few steps away. "After reviewing Morgan's most recent echocardiogram and EKG, she appears to be deteriorating more quickly than expected."

As a trained nurse, Mina had a sinking feeling. Clasping her hands together to comfort herself, Mina took in a breath. "What is your prognosis?" she asked with hesitation.

"My team and I estimate that Morgan has less than six months to live unless she receives a heart transplant. Given her current condition, I'm confident she will move up on the transplant list, but we won't know for certain for a couple of days," said the doctor.

"Will Morgan be able to go home soon?" asked Mina.

"I'm afraid not. At this moment, she would benefit from the watchful eye of our care team."

"I see," Mina softly replied as she processed her daughter's dismal outlook. The elevator chimed. Mina excused herself. "Thank you for the update."

In the hospital's grand lobby, Mina gravitated to a

vacant bench where 20-foot-tall glass windows over-looked the hospital's luscious greenery. Overwhelmed with decisions and uncertainties, she buried her head into her hands and sobbed.

CHAPTER 8

THE BACKROOM

G alen paced back and forth in front of his platform, pondering how he would pull off the unthinkable. The daunting task ahead, complicated by the looming exhibit departure, put Galen on edge.

"Galen! You're going to erode the marble." Still in a contemplative daze, Galen's temporal lobes[18] subconsciously processed the words before he could recognize who had uttered them. With the blink of an eye, Vitalis appeared in front of Galen, energized as ever.

"Wow! You look as jittery as me," Vitalis noted.

Galen's pensive mood and unease were impossible to hide.

"I know these past few days have been a lot to process, but take it from me, you'll settle in soon. You'll find a routine. I know what you need!" Vitalis exclaimed, fidgeting with a buzz of elation. "You should do something relaxing tonight. Give your mind a rest."

On the verge of Vitalis revealing his grand idea, Galen caught a glimpse of the whopping analog clock

---

[18] The temporal lobes are responsible for processing auditory information.

hanging over the exhibit's entrance. "It's time!" blurted Galen.

"Time for what?" Vitalis asked with a hint of confusion.

"Uh, to relax," Galen suggested, masking his intentions. "You know, you're right. I could use a diversion, something to ease my mind. I've been meaning to check out the jazz club. The smooth sounds of cool jazz with a hint of musical improv are just what the doctor ordered." Galen's comfort with his new persona was really growing on him.

"The jazz group calls themselves the *Tinnitus Sensations*. Be prepared. They'll keep your toe tapping all night, but they don't have the best sense of volume control." Vitalis scurried around the corner and out of sight.

Filled with a sense of conviction, Galen hurried to the jazz club. The others were already occupying a table in the back corner, stage right. Excusing himself, Galen made his way through the crowd of local fans who congregated near the front as the Tinnitus Sensations finished their last tuning progression. When Galen saw the external auditory meatuses[19] of all five musicians were filled with hardened plastinate fixatives, it became evident why the band was notorious for its loud music.

Galen greeted the others at the table. Marcel's eyes glistened with excitement to begin the evening. Taking advantage of the quiet interlude as the musicians settled in onstage, Marcel took the lead in the conversation.

---

[19] The external auditory meatus is the external opening of the ear canal which leads to the tympanic membrane (the eardrum).

"Now that we're all here, I think it's best to speak some-where a bit more secluded, for precautionary measures." Marcel threw back his head to finish his drink and then gingerly arose from the table as the drums and alto sax kicked off the first of a three-song set. Eyeing a covered doorway toward the back of the club no more than 15 feet away, he motioned to the group to follow him. Following suit, Cato, Cassius, Tome, and Galen stood up, pushed in their stools, and accompanied Marcel. Marcel held back a wall of thick black velvet curtains at the doorway to allow everyone passage into the backroom.

"While much of the plastination process focuses on displaying whole body preservations, the exhibit also likes to showcase isolated specimens," explained Cas-sius as they entered the seclusion of an atypical stock-room.

"Take a minute, Galen. Look around," insisted Mar-cel, as he stood in the middle of the small storage room filled with beautifully dissected specimens.

Large glass Kilner jars sat on sturdy metal shelves that lined the curious storeroom. Each contained a func-tioning organ submerged in formaldehyde. Galen roamed around the periphery of the room. The faint lub-dub of a beating heart that circulated the fluid from within its own jar caught Galen's attention and immedi-ately reminded him of Morgan. Galen marveled at the perfused lungs and watched as peristaltic waves rippled periodically through the walls of a suspended digestive tract. As he soaked in the wonderment of the spectacle, he could not help but feel he was being watched. Over his shoulder, Galen witnessed two glassy eyeballs with mesmerizing turquoise-blue irises following his every move.

While all the specimens were alluring in their own unique way, Galen was particularly fascinated by a delicate floating human fetus the size of a freshly picked pineapple. Galen inspected the fetus so closely that his nose almost touched the Kilner jar. At seven months gestation, all the developing human's miniature features were beautifully and wonderfully formed. The phenol solution that suspended the fetus swirled around its hand as it gestured a wave to Galen. With two fingers, Galen gestured a tiny wave in return.

"We'd better get to work before the Tinnitus Sensations call it a night," Tome urged.

"You're right," Marcel affirmed. "We need to reconnect Galen with Morgan and figure out how to get her the medication."

"My instinct is telling me that I need to get to Simon Floundary," Galen reasoned. "According to Arden, Dr. Floundary is already running a drug trial. Maybe I could convince him to enroll Morgan in the drug trial and to give her the medication."

"That is risky, but I agree it's our best shot at saving Morgan," Marcel admitted, though, he tended to agree with anything that screamed adventure.

"How are we going to locate Simon?" Galen asked. "I know Morgan is at Heidelberg University Hospital.

That's where she receives all her treatments. I heard the EKG when she answered yesterday."

"You're lucky Dr. Simon Floundary also conducts his research at Heidelberg University," Cato replied. "What would you have done if he worked in Munich?"

"But what's our current location?"

"We're in Heidelberg. At least that's what the gift shop t-shirts say," responded Marcel, who was once discovered secretly trying on gift-shop apparel.

"We'll have to determine the quickest route and mode of transportation to get to the university from here. I don't know our exact whereabouts, but I doubt we can walk there," Galen commented.

"What about the computer?" Cato interjected.

"What computer?" Cassius huffed, surprised by Cato's insider knowledge. Cassius prided himself on being the resourceful one of the bunch, at least from his perspective.

Cato waved the others over to a red and white fire escape plan hanging beside the velvet-covered doorway. "Here!" Cato shouted, a little too loudly while the Sensations were between songs. "It's in the plastination facility, room 817."

Cassius, resentful of Cato's quick thinking, hung back as the others pressed in to inspect the map. "How do you know?"

"A couple of weeks ago, I stayed overnight in the plastination room for cleaning and a touch-up. A rambunctious toddler tripped and spilled her sticky grape juice all over my gastrocnemius."[20] Cato pointed at a nearly invisible stain on his calf. "If we can get to the room, we'll be able to search for directions to the university."

Having a newfound sense of hope, Galen cheered, "That's brilliant! Let's go now." Like a herd of charging bison, the clan shuffled even closer to the velvet doorway. The music grew even louder.

"Hold your hyoids. It isn't that easy," Cassius stated, gripping Galen from behind bringing him back to reality. "We can't be seen by Arden, or the security guards for that matter."

"We can figure this out," Marcel replied. "Tome and Cassius can stay in the rotunda to keep watch. If you run into Arden, keep him occupied. Cato, Galen, and I will search the room and access the computer." Marcel paused and grimaced with deflated enthusiasm. "Wait. We don't have a key. The door is locked to secure the specimens and the valuable equipment."

Cassius put on his thinking face and repositioned his thick frames. As his lips parted, Galen beat him to the punch, "What about a key pick? There is a glass case full of old medical instruments on my platform. Maybe we could use them to pick the lock or to jimmy the door?"

"Exactly," grumbled Cassius to himself with a hint of annoyance.

The group shared a unanimous nod. It was settled.

---

[20] The gastrocnemius is the superficial most muscle of the calf that attaches to the calcaneus (heel bone) through the Achilles (calcaneal) tendon. This muscle is responsible for plantar flexion, the action demonstrated when walking on one's toes.

The five slipped out of the storage room, passed through the buzzing jazz club, and headed for Galen's platform. As the five-man crew darted past the poker table, Otto and Otis were at it again. This time, Galen overheard Otis say to Ivan, "Why didn't the skeleton eat the cafeteria food? Because he didn't have the stomach for it."

"Poor Ivan," Galen thought amid the roar of laughter from the duo. Though he wished he could intervene, at the moment his primary task was more important.

With a youthful leap onto the platform, Galen and Marcel scanned the glass case.

"Let's take the straight dental picks, the DeBakey forceps, the glass syringe, and curved mayo scissors," Galen suggested.

"Wow. Impressive," Cassius admired. "You're a quick study. It took me at least a week to be fluent in my new persona."

"I'm just reading the labels," Galen admitted unashamedly. He opened the lid and began stuffing the tools into a small turn-of-the-century doctor's bag made of black leather sitting adjacent to the display case.

"I think we're good to go. Good luck holding down the fort," Galen said, patting Tome on the back with enough force to throw his slices off balance. Galen glanced at Cassius and added, "Keep an eye out for Arden and, if need be, distract him."

CHAPTER 9

EXPOSED

Cato, Marcel, and Galen traversed the exhibit hall to the exit doors that led to the main hallway. Hyperaware of his surroundings, Galen scanned feverishly for security cameras, for which there were none. The building, and its caretakers, were far too antiquated for such technology. Never had Galen fully appreciated the angelic domed ceiling decorated with Renaissance crown molding and peach stenciled fleurs de lis that flowed seamlessly onto the walls. Two heavy black metal doors guarded the entryway marking their exit. At navel height, stainless steel panic bars outfitted each door for easy egress.

"Every night at closing, the guards patrol the exhibit halls only once and lock the doors externally behind them," Cato explained. "The doors remain locked all night until the morning rounds."

Marcel pressed gently on the crossbar jarring the door for a peek into the hallway. "We'll have to prop it open, so we're not locked out," he said.

Galen reached in and selected the needleless glass syringe from the doctor's bag. Once all three were in the hallway, he carefully positioned the syringe on the floor between the center doorpost and the door's edge.

They tip-toed down the long narrow hallway that flanked the exhibit hall. "It looks like...," The sound of distant footsteps synchronized to the harmony of jingling keys interrupted Cato's thought mid-sentence. "That's one of the night guards. We need to move fast! Room 817 is just down this hall. Third door on the left," Cato said frantically.

They scurried down the hall and counted as they passed each odd-numbered room. "817!" Galen whispered. "Quick, give me the tools!"

Marcel fumbled through the doctor's bag, searching for the dental picks. With instruments in hand, Galen felt alive. The familiarity and comfort of the tools cradled in his palm caught him by surprise. His new persona had taken over yet again. With the fine motor skills of a surgeon, he allowed his hands to be his guide. Marcel exchanged glances of doubt with Cato as Galen tinkered with the lock.

Five seconds elapsed. "Almost there...." Time had seemingly slowed to a crawl. "Hang tight." Marcel's nervous jittering bounce flustered Galen's concentration. If he could have held his breath, he would have.

Tensions mounted as the guard's footsteps approached from around the corner. The lock's tumbler finally let loose with a startling metallic click. The three flinched like a fan dodging a foul ball from behind a safety net. Instantly, Galen turned the knob and nudged open the door with his shoulder. The trio practically fell through the doorway and swiftly sealed the door behind them. Feeling an immense release of nervousness, Marcel shoved Galen off balance. "Wow! I feel alive! Way to go newbie." The three regrouped and turned their attention to their new surroundings.

"Welcome to the plastination room!" Marcel announced as if he owned the place. Metal tanks, basins of preservation fluid, and surgical instruments on Mayo stands filled the spacious room.

"Focus. We're here for the computer. Don't get absorbed by distractions," Cato ordered, revealing his Type-A personality.

"There's the computer." Galen pointed to a small wooden desk next to a coat rack adorned with lab coats.

Marcel developed a contemplative expression and began to strategize. "Let's divide and conquer. Cato, can you access the computer and get directions to the university? See what the options are for transportation."

Cato affirmed with a nod and took a seat at the desk. "I'll keep watch. Galen, see if there is anything that could come in handy for when we leave the museum. We may not have another chance to gather supplies."

Galen scoured the room, opening and closing every cabinet and drawer he could find. He considered a package of 3-0 silk sutures and tossed one item after another into his doctor's bag. Not fully aware of his surroundings, he backed into two 55-inch, pressurized gas tanks. The resounding clang of the aluminum cylinders sounded like dying church bells in need of repair. He quickly grasped one of the wobbling tanks with both palms to choke its reverberation. "Sorry! Carry on."

A partially opened drawer lured him to a gray filing cabinet. The drawer glides were stuck from years of wear and tear. He gave the drawer a heave to jar it open. Manila-colored folders filled the filing cabinet to the brim. Each file tab showed a handwritten name in black permanent marker. One folder sat slightly higher than all the others. It read *GALEN* in all caps. Though feeling pressed for time, he couldn't resist opening it. A summary of his past filled the record and gave Galen a welcomed reminder of the life he had suddenly left behind.

Age: *17*

Relationship Status: *Single*

Offspring Status: *No children*

Occupation: *High school student*

Medical History: *Non-union fracture reconstruction; Appendectomy*

Cause of Death: *Vehicular trauma; Innocent bystander*

At the sound of the printer taking in a fresh sheet of paper, Galen knew he couldn't waste any more time. He abruptly shut the folder, neatly placed it as he had found it, and began to close the drawer when he noticed Arden's file near the front of the stack. Galen's curiosity got the best of him. After glancing over his shoulder and side-stepping to obscure Marcel's view, he cracked open

Arden's file. Clipped to the cover sheet was an identification badge showing Arden as his former self. As he scanned the cover page, Galen found himself privy to every detail of Arden's past life.

Age: *62*

Relationship Status: *Married*

Offspring Status: *1 child*

Occupation: *Anatomy professor at Heidelberg University*

Medical History: *Hypertension; Inguinal hernia repair*

Cause of Death: *Myocardial infarction*

"Anatomy professor?" Galen was puzzled, yet not surprised. He replaced the folder to conceal his unintended discovery and glanced above the filing cabinet. A colorful poster of an anatomy mnemonic hung on display in front of him. His eyes fixated on the meticulously illustrated scapula. Above the illustration was a parody silhouette of soldiers watching a navy ship from a bridge. The poster read, '*The army (artery) goes over the bridge, the navy (nerve) goes under.*' Galen immediately recalled his conversation with Arden. Arden was not referencing his military expertise. He was referring to shoulder anatomy. How could an army lieutenant possess that kind of knowledge?

"I have the directions. You can get there by taking bus route 321. It will take you to the southeast corner of the campus," Cato said as he walked over to Galen who was standing in a speechless trance. "Galen, let's go! We can't dilly dally."

Marcel heard Cato's concerned tone and rushed over.

"I think Arden is different from us," asserted Galen. "Did you know he was an anatomy professor in his former life?"

"So, what's your point?" replied Marcel.

"What was your passion before death, Cato?" asked Galen.

"I don't recall," admitted Cato.

Galen quickly searched for Cato's file. "You were a chief financial officer and married with five children."

"Arden said that when we enter the plastinate realm, we take on our new persona. We lose our past memories and become ingrained in the role we're destined to maintain after death. I don't think this rule applies to Arden. When he took me to Nyla's mirror, he made it a point to note my shoulder's dissection and the surgical repair of my humerus. He rambled off a saying that no one without an anatomy background would ever understand. I think all of Arden's memories are intact."

"How could that be? All of us went through the same plastination process," Marcel chimed in.

"We need to get back to the exhibit," insisted Cato. "We'll sort this out later."

The trio headed for the door. "All we have to do is jog down the hallway and slip back into the exhibit. Easy peasy," Marcel remarked. "On three. One, two, three!"

They sprinted through the dimly lit corridor and refused to look back for fear of losing ground. Small, canned ceiling lights illuminated the entrance to the exhibit hall. Galen reclaimed the glass syringe that had propped open the exit door. A sense of relief and accomplishment flooded through his veins.

No more than ten steps beyond the entrance, the trio stiffened in their tracks at the sound of a startling yet familiar voice. "How nice of you two to show Galen the south side of the exhibit," said Arden. "I meant to give Galen the grand tour, but with Juno's delivery and the approaching move, I haven't had the chance."

Although their hearts no longer carried a productive beat, Galen, Cato, and Marcel felt their sympathetic nervous systems fire on hyperdrive. Given they could neither fight nor flee, Marcel stepped in. "Oh, don't worry about it, Arden. It's the least we could do. We know you have your hands full taking care of us and the exhibit," praised Marcel, who figured a little flattery was the best approach to covering their whereabouts.

"Let's go for drinks at the *Covered Hopper*," Galen chimed in, glancing at Arden with piercing eyes. "I haven't seen you take a break since I've been here."

Arden mulled it over and eventually agreed to join the others for a nightcap.

En route to the neighboring exhibit, a pamphlet tucked partway under a platform caught Galen's attention. "What's this?" He bent down to retrieve it.

"That's a map of the museum," answered Cato. "We find them lying about from time to time. The visitors are notorious for dropping them."

"Why don't you keep it?" Arden stated. "It would be good for you to learn about the museum's layout."

Galen agreed and slipped the map into his instrument tote. After all, the map might prove useful for strategizing their escape to hunt down Simon Floundary.

At the *Covered Hopper*, the trio, and their guest Arden, took a seat at the same table they occupied the night before. Each ordered a pint. For Galen, the brew was slightly more tolerable than the night before. After the first round, Galen ordered a second round of drinks for the entire group. "Let's have another. Doctor's orders."

Arden's demeanor grew more relaxed as he neared the end of the second pint of brew. His voice took on a lighter higher tone, and his personality became more jovial. Pleased with Arden's carefree disposition, Galen ordered a third round for good measure.

"Thank you for inviting me for drinks," Arden uttered slowly, trying not to slur his words. Arden was clearly a lightweight. "I must admit, while I enjoy my responsibilities in death, it takes a lot out of me. I can't believe I've been doing this for over three years. It seemed like only yesterday when I awoke for the first time after being plastinated."

"What was your plastination[21] experience like?" inquired Galen with malintent. "I, for one, recall feeling exposed and could never get comfortable."

"I found the acetone bath to be quite soothing," Arden reminisced. "However, since it removed all the water and fat in my body, getting out felt like leaving a hot tub. Luckily the forced impregnation of silicone rubber helped provide some insulation." Arden pushed his third pint, only a quarter full, to the growing glass collection at the center of the table. "The worst part for me was the curing stage. The gas used to solidify my position gave me a terrible headache for several days."

"Gas? Aren't we cured with heat?" Marcel queried, with a slight cock of his head.

"Heat. That's what I meant to say. We were all processed through the same plastination stages," assured Arden. "I think I've had too many drinks. No more for me tonight."

Galen, Cato, and Marcel quickly exchanged glances. They knew Arden was bluffing, given the change in his tone and his sloppy backpedaling.

"It's such a shame we lose our memories," Galen commented. "I feel mine slipping away. I can barely recall my childhood." Galen leaned back in his chair as if having just consumed an entire five-course meal. "I just hope in this life I'll feel the same joy and purpose I did when I helped people through my volunteer work." Looking straight at Arden, Galen went for the full-court

---

[21] Refer to the back matter of this book for an overview of the plastination process.

press, "I can only imagine how many students' lives you've impacted."

A subtle but observable smile overpowered Arden's ability to contain his joy at the thought of his beloved students. Despite wearing camouflage pants, Arden felt contrite and fully exposed. As quickly as Arden's smile appeared, he withdrew it into a ridged glare realizing Galen now owned his deepest secret.

CHAPTER 10

RELENTLESS

Before anyone had an opportunity to say a proper good night, Arden raced down the dining car's stairs. An expression of disdain drew his brows toward the bridge of his nose. The thought of his past and current state being fully exposed consumed Arden with angst. His hastened gait carried him out of sight before the others could reach the egress of the *Covered Hopper*.

"We need his help!" Galen petitioned Cato and Marcel, who were now also convinced Arden had been concealing more information than they had ever realized. "If his memories are as clear as we think, then his knowledge of the university could help us reach Simon Floundary." Replete with unease, Galen clung to the hope that Arden's memories and perceptivity would be his saving grace. Struck by the wistful thought of Morgan's enduring fight for her life, Galen rushed back to the table to grab his tote and gave chase to Arden.

"Arden!" Galen shouted in every direction as he searched the exhibit hall weaving in and out of the displays. He scoured every platform and systematically panned the mundane crowd of the walking dead. At last, Galen spotted Arden readjusting Hippos' saddle at the far side of the hall.

"Good boy," Galen heard Arden murmur as he patted the stead's flank and proceeded to tighten the straps around the horse's girth.

"Arden, I need your help. There is only a short time left," Galen panted as if he was out of breath, though his pleural cavities were barren. "With your memory of the university, you can help us reach Simon Floundary before it's too late. Please! You're my only hope to save Morgan." Galen's panting faded to a crackled but genuine plea. "I can't save her without you."

"I imagine that I've come across as insensitive to your desire to save your junior flame," Arden stated, acknowledging Galen, who still blushed at Arden's choice of words. "I have deep empathy for you and Morgan." Arden took a pregnant pause to clear his intoxicated mind. He squatted on a three-legged stool meant for Hippos' caretaker to subdue his dizziness. "The wealth of information we hold as the custodians of biomedical knowledge is staggering. I would love for nothing more than to share the cure for cancer and every other disease with the world. But with the privilege of this knowledge comes the responsibility to disclose it at its appointed time, only to those who are open and ready to receive it."

"I understand the significance of our gift and fully realize the risks," Galen interjected like any other teenager trying to convince the world of his maturity. "I promise to uphold the Code of Silence, for my own well-being and that of others. Failure is not an option."

"And how do you plan to do that?" Arden scrutinized. "You're just an emotionally inept juvenile incapable of expressing your feelings. Is this about Morgan or about you? Your old life is complete, no matter how short-lived it was. There are no more opportunities to tell Morgan how you feel. That ship has sailed. And you're not the invincible superhero you think you are." Galen dropped his shoulders and turned away deflated. Arden backed down realizing his extreme temperament.

"There are many individuals I long to see and help from my past life," Arden continued with caution, "but we cannot wittingly defy the order entrusted to us. I am in a position where I place myself, and those I am responsible for, at risk if I offer assistance. If my secret is revealed to the others, there could be a mutiny among the bodies; an unrelenting pursuit for knowledge of their former selves." Hippos whinnied and nudged his snout against Galen's neck. "Even worse, the perils of envy among the ranks may breed a disregard for our kind's safety and the wellbeing of those who benefit from our wisdom. Your yearning to help Morgan is unprecedented." Arden slid over to the next platform to mend the crossbar of a fence post that had fallen. "You remind me of a terribly annoying and relentless student I once had."

"Oh, really? How so?" Galen reluctantly prodded, only half interested.

"It's not relevant," stated Arden with a wave of his hand signaling the end of their conversation.

"No, really! How am I anything like your student? You don't even know me," Galen mustered up an ounce of courage to fight back, pressing Arden like a trial witness. "I'm a kind and caring introvert who would do anything to save my best friend. How can you even think to compare me to one of your pretentious students?"

Arden sternly turned to face Galen, who uncontrollably glanced at the floor. Arden's eyes glanced off into the distance. "His name was Liam. He was in my undergraduate anatomy dissection class. One day, he came to my office begging me to sponsor a club he wanted to start on campus. The club helped to organize international mission trips to third-world countries for students aspiring to practice medicine." Arden refocused his gaze to look Galen in the eyes. "Before Liam even outlined the responsibilities, I knew it would be more work than I was willing to commit to. Not to mention the possible financial obligations. I didn't want to be that faculty member who always asked for donations at department meetings. Nor did I feel equipped to oversee the mission trips he envisioned." Arden placed his hand against Hippos to steady himself against the nightcap's effects. He nodded to an elderly kyphotic woman passing by dragging a stubborn goat in tow. "Being held responsible for a handful of college students in a foreign country made me very uneasy and was not my idea of a good time. Even after expressing my reservations, Liam wouldn't take no for an answer. Day after day, for five weeks straight, he delivered a handwritten letter to my office mailbox explaining how I was the best person to sponsor his start-up. He would end each letter by writing, 'Give me one chance to change one life. Be the difference.'" Arden moved on to another platform to tidy up the next display.

"Wait! What happened? Did you agree to be the sponsor?" Galen nudged, fully consumed by the story.

"Well, yes. I mean, it was either that or I would have continued to receive letters from Liam until he graduated. The kid's heart was as big as the moon and in the right place. I softened up to him and agreed to help. In hindsight, I'm glad I did. We organized a mission trip to the Dominican Republic three years in a row. During our time there, we provided blood pressure screenings, worked alongside doctors, and helped the locals to better understand the importance of health education. Every mission trip was always more gratifying and humbling than I imagined."

"My intentions are no different than Liam's. All I want is to help Morgan," Galen urged. "You stepped out of your comfort zone for Liam. Now, I'm asking you to be the linchpin of our mission. Be the difference, just once more. Morgan's life hangs in the balance. Isn't a girl's hope for a brighter future worth supporting?"

Arden picked up a plastic apple from a teacher's desk on display and buffed it to a sheen against his camouflaged trousers. The conundrum weighed heavily on him. "Your escape may never be made known to the others. You must accept full responsibility for all risks involved."

"I do. I accept full responsibility for anything that happens."

"If you fail by exposing yourself and our kind, you will perish indefinitely. The Council of Corpses has no tolerance for such behavior. This is not a decision to take lightly. Though your youthful spirit is inspiring, you'll need more than compassion for your cause to prevail. You'll need wisdom beyond your years, bravery, ingenuity, and integrity."

"You've seen how quickly my new persona has taken hold. I'm confident that with my new abilities, I can navigate any challenge and overcome any obstacle. I'm ready to mingle with the living to be the difference."

"I will help you on one condition. You must guarantee that what you and your comrades know about me will remain between us. It must never be spoken of again. Are we in agreement?" Arden asked in a tone as serious as a judge delivering a conviction verdict.

"Your secret is safe with us," Galen assured, knowing he could only speak for himself.

Arden dutifully extended his hand to Galen. As a lump formed at the back of Galen's oropharynx, he pulled Arden in close for a vibrant unexpected embrace. "That's enough, soldier," Arden asserted as he peeled himself from Galen's affectionate squeeze. "Meet me in the cartography room at zero six hundred hours."

"Yes, sir!" Galen stood at attention, feeling like an army cadet preparing for a special mission.

"Should I invite the others to join us?" Galen suggested.

Arden adamantly shook his head *no* at his atlantoaxial joint.[22] "It's too risky. From this point forward, we must keep all communications to a minimum." Galen nodded in agreement as Arden turned and walked away.

Standing alone in isolation, processing the significance of what had just happened, Galen realized he had no idea where the cartography room was located. Though he wished he could race to Cato and Marcel to share the exciting news, he knew keeping his word was more important. Instead, Galen strolled to a nearby park bench beneath a large faux tree. He took a seat opposite the shadow created by the overhanging artificial foliage. He sat his leather tote on the bench's green-painted slats and pulled out the museum map he had found earlier. Galen expanded the map to see every visible crease. He charted an invisible course to the cartography room with his finger. He hesitated when he learned the cartography room was adjacent to the *Revenge of the Pharaohs* exhibit. Uncomfortable flashbacks of the preservation process surfaced without warning. Galen's mind began to wander. "Do the mummies awake each night too?" He shuddered at the thought of encountering a decayed 6,000-year-old mummy. Normally, the thought would have given him goosebumps, but he no longer had skin or hair follicles.

---

[22] The atlantoaxial joint is the articulation between the atlas (the first cervical vertebra) and the axis (the second cervical vertebra). This joint permits head rotation, thus allowing an individual to shake his or her head 'No'.

Galen intently digested all the museum had to offer. He found the *Underground Expedition* exhibit quite intriguing. A photo showed a series of dimly lit corridors lined from wall to ceiling with a rocky façade. He thought it was reminiscent of the bony facial canal he recalled seeing in his persona manual. The exhibit gave visitors the full experience of tunneling underground as they walked through the mining industry's history. A closer investigation of the *Underground Expedition* revealed it had two exits. One exit led to the *Grainger Hall of Gems*. Galen smirked at the thought of Morgan's rough blue diamond. That was his favorite gift he had ever gotten for her. The second exit, not intended for the public, led to an outdoor play area. In the adjacent photo, an assortment of miniature digging equipment for children to climb on inundated the play yard. In one section of the yard, children used hand tools to excavate hidden treasures in the triple-ground mulch. It was clear that the museum went above and beyond to provide its visitors with the most immersive of experiences.

Having lost track of time, Galen glanced at the clock. The minute hand crept to the eleventh position. He had five minutes to find the cartography room for his meeting with Arden.

Galen cautiously peered out from behind the exhibit door before fully committing the rest of his body. He glided, as silent as falling snow, past a wall of arched windows. Halfway along the corridor, he stood deadlocked at a metal encased door that read, *Stairs. Fire exit only. Alarm will sound.*

"So much for meticulously planning a route," Galen murmured to himself. Dumbfounded by his poor planning, he quickly consulted the museum map to locate the nearest elevator. Meandering through the hallway like the tortuous course of the splenic artery, he turned the corner, finally locating his plan B. The lift's doors were shut tighter than the tonic constriction of the stomach's pyloric sphincter. Galen's finger repeatedly jabbed at the elevator button in a nervous triplet pattern like a woodpecker. He watched as the numbers sluggishly climbed from the sixth to the eighth floor. The loud high-pitched ding indicating the elevator's arrival threw Galen into a momentary panic. Like an elusive fugitive, he dashed to the far side of a soda vending machine, just out of view of the elevator's doors. As the doors drew open, he prayed no one would exit. The elevator was empty.

"Third floor," Galen recalled with a whisper as he firmly engaged the round ivory button trimmed in tarnished bronze. With a slight unexpected jerk, the elevator heaved and began its descent. Seven, six, five. As the fourth floor neared, the lift slowed to a screeching halt. Terrified, Galen swiveled with an about-face fixing his eyes on the accumulated dust in the corner of the elevator car. He stood as motionless as a tree stump. The old aluminum doors stuttered open.

CHAPTER 11

THE PLEXUS

An unnerving voice rang out like an alarm bell. "What are you up to?" Unsure of whether to speak, weep, or run, Galen stood stationary in the cozy corner of the elevator car paralyzed by fear. He was lucky his bowels were not functioning.

"You know I can see you, right?" the voice rang out again. Galen slowly turned more nervous than when he almost kissed Morgan, only to find Marcel.

Galen breathed an audible sigh of relief as his hand covered his chest. "I suppose the expression, 'You scared me to death,' no longer applies," Galen remarked resorting to humor to slow the sudden adrenaline surge. "What are you doing here?"

"I saw you slip away, and I followed you. When I saw you get on the elevator, I couldn't resist a little prank."

"How did you get to the fourth floor so quickly?"

"I took the stairs," said Marcel as if it was a dumb question.

"But the sign said the alarm would sound."

"There has never been an alarm on that door. The museum staff put that sign there to deter visitors from taking the stairs. The old handrails are not up to fire code," Marcel stated as if it was common knowledge. "Where are you headed, anyway?"

"I'm meeting Arden in the cartography room," Galen blurted without thinking.

"He agreed to help!" squealed Marcel with excitement. "Bravo!" He began to clap obnoxiously.

"Yes, but you can't tell anyone," Galen replied in a hushed tone motioning for Marcel to calm down.

"I'm coming with you," said Marcel.

"No, you can't!"

"I'm coming with you."

"You can't. I promised Arden," pleaded Galen.

"Great, then it's settled. I'm coming with you," Marcel persisted.

"What? No!" Galen responded more forcefully, confused as to why he was not getting through to Marcel.

"You need a wingman. And we need code names," Marcel continued in his own little world of a mission impossible fantasy. "Ooouuu, maybe we'll dangle from a safety line to climb a tall building," fantasized Marcel.

"Marcel, I'm late, thanks to your little prank. I have to meet Arden if we stand a chance at helping Morgan." Galen grew more impatient.

"Follow me," said Marcel.

Feeling he had no other choice, Galen reluctantly followed Marcel to the stairwell. They descended one flight of stairs, took a left at a small coffee stand inside the 3rd-floor lobby, walked past the entrance to the *Revenge of the Pharaohs* exhibit, and hung a right at the colossal wooly mammoth replica sporting impressive, bowed ivory tusks.

"Here we are," said Marcel as if he was ending a guided tour.

Ahead, a glass wall partitioned off the temperature-regulated cartography room from the rest of the grandiose museum. Four feet from the ground, the frosted glass wall faded to clear glass. The sleek modern design beautifully complimented the museum's historic charm. On a brick-clad column, next to the glass door, hung a bronze nameplate reading *Cartography: Room 300*. Inside, Arden hunched over a case as he carefully inspected a map with his back to the glass panes.

Galen paused outside the room. The glass door with chrome-plated hinges was guarded by a numbered keypad. Galen flinched when he looked up from the keypad. Like a scene straight from a horror film, Arden stood peering at him face-to-face from behind the glass. His stern eyes pinned Galen to the wall. Galen peered over his shoulder. Marcel was just out of Arden's sight performing a callisthenic warm-up near the entrance to the *Revenge of the Pharaohs* exhibit. If it weren't for the caution tape indicating the exhibit's construction, Marcel would have probably scaled the faux pyramid's face just to prove a point.

Galen regained his composure and returned his attention to Arden. Arden slowly and deliberately signed four numbers. 1...2...2...9. Recognizing he was supposed to follow along, Galen quickly punched in the four digits and watched the small LED light change from red to green. Cranking the handle, Galen slid smoothly through the doorway as though lubricated by synovial fluid and softly closed the glass panel behind him.

Framed prints of late 18th-century Heidelberg maps, arranged by decade, adorned the blueberry-colored walls. Display cases bordering the periphery housed and protected the more delicate and smaller authentic maps. As Galen took in his surroundings, he noticed an 1830s map that showed the intersecting crossroads of his grandparent's home. "Wow, would you look at that," said Galen. "There's the street where I learned to ride a bike."

Across the room, Arden gently opened the top drawer of an antique wooden cabinet. Intrigued to see what was inside, Galen rushed to peer over his shoulder.

"The maps in this cabinet are organized by German state," Arden explained. He lifted a thick folder and laid it atop the neighboring display case. Quickly flipping through the various maps and blueprints, Arden exuded a level of energy that Galen had never witnessed before. "Here!" Arden announced as he laid out a bound set of plans in front of them.

Arden sifted through the stack of bound prints.

"These are the blueprints for the university. Each academic building has its own page." As Arden uncovered relevant prints, he set them to the side. Galen picked up a print from the top of the pile. In the lower right-hand corner, in a dusty gray script, the print read *Department of Medical Sciences*. The scaphoid-shaped[23] building had six floors.

"What a sight," Arden admired. "That building was practically my second home." He pointed to a small square on the fourth floor, "This was my office. This larger section, just down the south hallway, is the cadaver lab."

"Where do you think Simon Floundary's lab is?" Galen asked anxiously.

"Presuming things haven't changed, the pathology lab is here." Arden pointed to an office space on the second floor of the same building. "Given Simon's newer clinical research focus, his office and lab may have moved closer to the medical center. The medical cadavers will know exactly where his office is located."

"Here are the stairs and elevator next to the cadaver lab," Arden pointed. "This elevator also goes to the sub-basement and connects with a plexus of underground tunnels."

"A tunnel system?" Galen's stapedius muscle[24] constricted, startled by the volume of his own voice. The

---

[23] The scaphoid bone is the largest of the eight carpal bones of the wrist. When bearing weight on one's hand, the scaphoid bone transmits the force to the radius, the weight bearing bone of the forearm. As such, a fall on an outstretched hand, referred to as a FOOSH injury, can cause a scaphoid fracture.

[24] The stapedius muscle is the smallest skeletal muscle in the human body measuring approximately 1mm in length. The stapedius muscle dampens vibrations of the stapes (the smallest of the three ear

notion of a tunnel system caught him off guard.

"Yes, the labyrinth is a work of art!" stated Arden. "The university built steam tunnels during World War II for protection from possible airstrikes and to convey utilities more efficiently between campus buildings. In the post-war era, the tunnels primarily served as an alternative to braving the frigid cold during the winter months. The administration proposed closing the tunnels to save on regular maintenance costs, but the Department of Medical Sciences objected. By this route, all cadavers are transported, out of the public's view, from the medical center morgue and embalming facility to the student laboratory."

Arden grabbed another blueprint from the pile which looked to be an enlarged copy of the buildings' tunnel connections. "Your best option is to capitalize on the tunnel plexus. The medical center acts as the central node where all the tunnels converge. There are a total of only three entrances into the tunnel system, all of which are restricted by keycard access. In addition, five steam grates double as emergency exits. One afternoon, I was transporting bodies with two of my graduate students when an alarm in the tunnels sounded. We were ushered by security to the nearest exit at one of the steam grates. We had to engage a spring lever to release and open the grate."

"How will I gain entry to the tunnel if the release mechanism is internal?" Galen questioned.

---

ossicles and smallest bone in the body) against the oval window to protect the inner ear from loud external noises.

"The grates' slots are wide enough that you'll be able to lower a loop of fishing line to yank on the lever. You'll need to grab the fishing line from the plastination room. You may even need to create a braided rope of line to improve its tensile strength," recommended Arden.

"Good idea."

Arden continued, "The cadaver lab is in the Medical Sciences building which sits at the southeast corner of the campus. About 300 feet away is the closest grate just outside the Center of Molecular Biology building. This is where you'll want to enter the tunnel plexus."

"I wish I was writing this down. Is there anything else I should know?" questioned Galen.

"You'll also need my ID badge to access the anatomy lab," Arden stated.

It was hard for Galen to contain his excitement. Getting to Simon Floundary was finally within reach. Just as quickly as his emotions swelled, the onslaught of overwhelming logistics stifled his enthusiasm. He realized he still did not know how he would get Morgan the medication or register her for the drug trial.

"What am I doing?" Galen said aloud, dejected. The self-doubt of impostor syndrome had raised its ugly head. "I don't know where the medication is stored. I don't know how to access the trial database. This mission may be nothing but a lost cause." Galen berated his own capabilities as his confidence waned.

"I believe the secret to this mission's success lies in

the cadaver lab at Heidelberg University. The information you need resides with the medical cadavers. If you explain everything to them and convince them of your need for Ribozore, perhaps they'll be willing to reveal pertinent information sooner than intended," Arden proposed.

Galen nodded his head in agreement. "Will you come with me? Instead of relying on this information, why don't you come too? It will be a walk down memory lane."

"Wouldn't that be something," Arden said, pondering Galen's offer. "But I can't leave my responsibilities here. With the move quickly approaching, there is far too much to do in preparation. I must also prepare for the new arrivals. Acclimating a new platoon of specimens to this new life is a duty I hold dear to my heart."

"Wait. Are you saying you won't be coming with us to the next museum?" Galen gasped.

"That's right, but I'm used to it. It reminds me of my experience with each new cohort of budding medical students. I took them in, taught them everything I knew, and then sent them off, encouraging them to face their new world and responsibilities with confidence. As they left their training, I prayed they would accomplish far greater things than I could ever achieve on my own. I feel the same way about all of you," Arden admitted.

This insight gave Galen a newfound appreciation and respect for Arden. "Thank you, Arden, for your leadership," Galen remarked with sincerity.

"May I take these blueprints for reference?" Galen asked, knowing they may prove useful.

"I suppose, but don't lose them. We'll need to return the prints before someone realizes they're missing."

Scanning the room, Arden found an old, elongated canister tucked away in the corner next to the wooden flat-drawer file cabinet. Galen meticulously rolled up the blueprints. Arden carefully slid the prints into the tube and situated the cylinder snuggly in his axilla. "We should get back," Arden said, feeling dawn's approach.

They opened the glass door and scanned the main hallway just beyond the alcove. Galen and Arden leisurely walked past the *Revenge of the Pharaohs* exhibit toward the nearest elevator.

"I have to ask," Galen said timidly. "Do the mummies...you know?"

Arden chuckled. "No," he stated emphatically. "Ancient Egyptian preservation techniques, while impressive, never had the right combination of chemicals to awaken the pharaohs. Besides, how would they release knowledge of scientific advances while sealed within a sarcophagus and limestone tomb?" Galen absorbed the information unable to argue against the logic.

"How long have cadavers been the gatekeepers of scientific knowledge?"

Delighted by the genuineness of the question, Arden elaborated, "As early as the 3rd century B.C., ancient Greek physicians dissected and interacted with cadavers. A fluid, unregulated flow of scientific information from our kind to early physicians, scientists, and philosophers was commonplace until the incident of 1564. Out of necessity, the Council of Corpses urgently authorized and executed the Code of Silence, among other codes. Andreas Vesalius, a seminal physician and anatomist, disclosed his intimate workings and interactions with cadavers to the public. Our world, for the first and only time, became exposed, putting us in grave danger. The Council of Corpses disavowed Vesalius and painted him as a madman. It was the only way to regain control of the information entrusted to the cadaver world. The Council has enacted the Code of Silence ever since."

As Galen reached to call the elevator, the museum's intercom system broadcasted an announcement. "The museum will open in thirty minutes. Unlock the doors to each exhibit." A sustained beep followed the rusty voice.

Arden grabbed Galen's arm and quickly yanked him into the lift. "We must return, immediately, before the guard unlocks the doors. If he hears the bodies before they set, they'll be discovered."

Galen did not know how to react. Arden was always so calm and collected. When the elevator doors sprung open, Arden and Galen raced down the eighth-floor hallway with a Vitalis-like vigor. Gliding through the corridor, they exercised stealth yet maintained a hurried pace. Arden flung open the exhibit's door while Galen scooped up the syringe door prop.

"Get to your platforms, everyone!" Arden declared

as he entered the room. Arden handed Galen the blueprints in their protective canister and bolted away for a final round of checks.

"Galen!"

Galen whipped around. Marcel hurried over to meet him. Galen lifted the tube like a trophy. "I have the prints!" he exclaimed. I'll catch everyone up to speed tomorrow."

Marcel confirmed with a nod and a stinging high-five before he darted back to his display. Marcel's platform modeled a petite garden fence with shrubs and flowers on either side. He liked to demonstrate his athleticism by striking his moritati pose in mid-air as he bounded over the fence using only one arm to steady himself. He liked to joke that he was fleeing from an enraged protective father after kissing his secret lover goodnight. Of course, everyone knew this was merely another figment of Marcel's creative imagination.

A sense of chaos filled the atmosphere in Arden's temporary absence. Arden judiciously worked to orchestrate a smooth transition to opening. While Vitalis tried to tame his ostrich, Otto and Otis called antes. Ivan, with his jaw cradled in his palm, had already folded.

Galen looked across at Marcel and gestured a wink. With all that had transpired that evening, Galen knew tomorrow would be pivotal. It would be his only chance to be the difference.

As Arden took his final position, Galen mouthed,

"Thank you." Arden tipped his brow in return. At Arden's command, their stances solidified, and their eyes glazed over. Everything went dark.

CHAPTER 12

Heartstrings

A kind and friendly receptionist called out to the waiting room, "Dr. and Mrs. Floundary? Dr. Cramer will see you now."

Simon Floundary and his wife, Elena, left the quiet comfort of the waiting room to follow the receptionist. Despite their looks of uncertainty and concern, they optimistically hoped for good news. The receptionist stopped halfway down the hallway. She motioned for the couple to enter the office suite, and announced, "The Floundary family is here to see you, doctor."

Dr. Cramer, who was pushing retirement age, invited Simon and Elena into his well-manicured office. "Hello and thank you for coming. It's nice to see you again." He stood behind a cherry Elizabethan-style writing desk as he obligatorily greeted the couple. His caramel-colored sports coat complemented his chiffon white hair combed neatly to the side; what was left of it anyway. His sagging jowls added length to his already long face. Formal introductions were not necessary. The Floundarys had already interacted closely with Dr. Cramer on multiple occasions. He had diagnosed their son several weeks prior.

"Please make yourselves comfortable," Dr. Cramer said as he motioned to Simon and Elena to take a seat on a couch in the sitting area of his plush office. The leather Chesterfield sofa faced a wall of inset bookshelves lined with neurosurgery textbooks, journals, trinkets, and the occasional family photo. Opposite the couch were two ornate armchairs upholstered with a subtle brocade pattern. Dr. Cramer settled himself towards the front of one of the chairs. He sat tall and leaned in as he spoke.

"Thank you for meeting with me today. As you know, tomorrow afternoon will be a very critical day for your son, Jesse. I would like to take time to discuss the procedure he'll be undergoing. I would also like to answer any questions you may have." Dr. Cramer skipped the congenial small talk and cut straight to the specifics. His tight clinical schedule necessitated efficiency and never allowed enough time for the relational or humanistic aspects of medicine.

"Because of the location of Jesse's tumor, we'll be taking a suboccipital approach to access it. If you feel the bump on the back of your head at the base of your skull, that is the external occipital protuberance.[25] We will be inserting instruments through an opening that we create just beneath this bump. After we navigate past his upper cervical vertebrae and into the large skull base opening called the foramen magnum,[26] we'll be in the location where we can begin to visualize the tumor." Dr. Cramer clasped his hands together as if giving himself

---

[25] The external occipital protuberance is the palpable bump at the base of the posterior skull.
[26] The foramen magnum is the large opening in the base of the skull that transmits the spinal cord to the vertebral canal.

moral support. "I think it goes without saying, but I want to emphasize that brain surgery is highly invasive. It comes with several risks." Simon, not entirely ready to absorb operative details, needed smaller morsels of information and a longer processing time. Dr. Cramer, however, was clearly on autopilot and was not about to switch over to manual. He barreled forward. "For example, an iatrogenic injury resulting from the surgery could lead to breathing and swallowing impairments or even vocal cord incoordination. Given the seriousness of Jesse's condition, this procedure could also result in his death, if there are complications."

After the *death bomb*, Dr. Cramer finally paused to allow the gravity of the conversation to fully settle. Yet, it was too late. The bomb had already inflicted havoc on two casualties. Simon and Elena stared into a hollow abyss, shell-shocked. Overwhelmed, they sat stock-still not knowing what questions to ask or how to respond. Only an act of God could have stirred them from their trance.

Dr. Cramer slowly and deliberately spoke with the endearing tenderness that both Simon and Elena needed. "I realize you've never experienced a situation like this before, but..." It was the dreaded incendiary *'but'*. The momentary comfort Simon and Elena felt from Dr. Cramer's perfunctory empathy vanished as the already bleak conversation unexpectedly turned course, again. "I want to make certain you are prepared for the worst outcome." Elana gripped Simon's hand even tighter. "Before procedures like these, it is my professional duty and obligation to educate patients and their families about the impact of organ and whole-body donation." Dr. Cramer pushed forward without reading the room's tentativeness. "When it comes to organ donation, a single donor can donate up to eight life-saving organs. When considering corneas and other tissues, a single donor could improve the lives of up to 75 individuals. Jesse's blood type is O-negative, meaning his organs could be donated to individuals with any blood type."

Dr. Cramer took another brief pause, though, at this point in the conversation, the pregnant pause had lost all effect. Simon repositioned himself in his seat, no longer wanting to look Dr. Cramer in the eyes. Dr. Cramer lingered on the topic like a student phlebotomist repeatedly sticking a patient to find the perfect vein and needle position. "Alternatively, whole-body donation is the act of donating an entire body to advance the cause of science and education. In some instances, one individual may be both an organ and a whole-body donor."

Simon's fidgeting body language affirmed his unease with the conversation. His left knee quivered with trepidation.

"It is my sincerest hope that you will never have to decide whether your son should be a donor. My team and I commit to giving Jesse the best care that we can provide." Dr. Cramer's sincere reassurance came far too late in the conversation to yield any meaningful effect. "Is there anything I can clarify?"

Elena turned to Simon waiting for her husband to

speak. Simon wore his deep discomfort on his expressionless face. Given Simon's background, he typically took the lead in all medically related conversations. This time, he said nothing as he costively processed Dr. Cramer's words.

Elena spoke up instead. "That's certainly a lot of information to consume. We have no questions at the moment. Thank you for your time." Elena nudged Simon who managed only half of an artificial smile. Simon bolted straight to the door leaving Elena behind to catch up as she gathered her purse.

An eerie lull of complete silence saturated the drive home from Dr. Cramer's office. The thought of Jesse's risky procedure perturbed Simon, especially. It represented an irreversible decision they would have to live with for the rest of their lives, for better or for worse.

When they arrived home in the driveway, Elena spoke first, "My mom said she would stay with Jesse through the night if we wanted." She waited for Simon to answer, but only the sound of the transmission shifting into park responded to her question. Simon reached to the rear seat to grab his messenger bag and engaged the handle of the driver's door, intentionally ignoring Elena.

"You've not said a word since we left the doctor's office. What's on your mind?" Elena probed. "You're stewing about something." Elena saw right through the intangible shield Simon hid his emotions behind.

"I cannot believe the doctor blindsided us like that to talk about donating our son's organs as if he'll never make it through the surgery." Simon raised his voice, suddenly unleashing a well of frustration. "I know the procedure carries more risk than most, but as an already concerned parent, I do not need this extra burden right now. It's mental torture to think we could lose our only child tomorrow, and that the doctor wants to cannibalize him for parts." Simon writhed waving his fist through the air as if planning to strike something.

"I'm just as scared as you are. I'm worried stiff," affirmed Elena. "Dr. Cramer was doing his job. You can't fault him for that or take this out on him."

"I'm not ready for this," roared Simon.

"No one ever is," consoled Elena, "But we need to be prepared just in case. What do you think we should do?"

"I don't want to donate his organs," Simon decisively stated.

"It sounds like you've already made up our minds," Elena replied snidely.

"I have!" asserted Simon hoping his authoritative stance would annihilate the conversation.

"He is my son too, and I love him just as much as you do," countered Elena. "Don't I get a say in this decision? And what about Jesse? Perhaps he should have a say."

"We are not mentioning this to Jesse. When he leaves for surgery, the only things I want on his mind are positive thoughts and the hope that he'll pull through this."

"All of this is tugging at my heartstrings, too," Elena confessed. "I think we should donate his organs if it comes to that. You know as well as I do that Jesse is compassionate about helping those in need. He has the biggest heart of any child I know. If he was of age to decide for himself, I'm certain he would choose to donate," Elena argued on Jesse's behalf.

"I cannot bear the thought of having pieces of him ripped out to live on in someone else," Simon explained. "I could never have closure if that happened."

"This isn't about you, Simon! It doesn't matter how comfortable you are with death or whether you'll ever get closure. What matters is Jesse and his legacy."

Fed up with the quarrel, Simon stormed inside. Elena followed in pursuit. "After I grab a bite for dinner, I'm going to the hospital to be with Jesse," said Elena as Simon continued to physically distance himself by heading to the bedroom.

"I need to trim the lawn. The grass looks horrendous," Simon yelled from the landing. He went straight to the closet to change out of his dress clothes and into workout shorts. Elena had seen this behavior in Simon before when his mother passed away from ovarian cancer. His modus operandi was to do everything in his power to distance himself from reality, including devising excuses and prioritizing the lowliest of tasks to sideline any uncomfortable conversation.

Elena left for the hospital disappointed in her husband and his inability to move beyond his own conceit. The remainder of the evening, Simon buried himself in miscellaneous chores and lingering office work, all of which he felt were perfectly justifiable distractions.

After spending quality time with Jesse, Elena left him in the care of her mother. She intended to return home, hoping Simon had calmed his demeanor. Alone with her thoughts in the car, her home was the last place she wanted to be. She did all she could to hold herself together. No matter how emotionally strong she was, she could not suppress the thought of her son undergoing a risky but necessary procedure.

At a familiar stoplight three blocks from her neighborhood, Elena impulsively turned the car in the opposite direction. Within minutes, she found herself outside of a dear friend's residence. Elena knocked softly on the front door with a hint of hesitation, knowing the children would be fast asleep. Her bestie answered in a white plush robe with a vexed look. Upon recognizing Elena as the unannounced visitor, her expression changed to one of genuine sympathy and concern.

"Did I crash your romantic movie marathon?" Elena asked blushing, feeling a bit contrite for not calling ahead. As any true friend would, the woman in the white robe welcomed Elena inside and with wide open arms greeted her with a hug. Over the next hour, Elena confided in her close friend for the impassioned support she desperately needed but knew Simon could never offer. Having an open non-combative discussion is all Elena wanted to help reach her own conclusions.

When Elena finally returned home, Simon had already retired for the night. His subtle almost rhythmic snoring indicated he was fast asleep. The covers were drawn tight over his shoulders leaving Elena hardly any blankets. Elena discreetly slipped into bed. Her heart-strings were tied in knots as she questioned whether Jesse's surgery was the right decision. The one thing she knew for certain was that she would have to move mountains to change Simon's mind. While Simon's tenacious attitude was one of the reasons Elena married him, in times like this, his stubbornness was hardly bearable.

CHAPTER 13

OPERATION BUSM

Seven hours until crating.

Tap, tap, tap. Galen awoke to Tome poking him on the forehead. "Rise and shine! We have a big day ahead of us," Tome grinned.

"Where's Marcel?" Galen asked, seeing his platform was vacant.

"He's rounding up the others. He asked me to wake you, seeing as your sleep cycle is still off." Galen rolled his neck from one shoulder to the other to shake his stiffness. "It sounds like you had quite the evening with Arden."

"Yes. It was very productive. Arden let me borrow the university maps." He crouched on his hands and knees to retrieve the tube from under his platform where he had securely hidden it. "To pull this off in a single night, we'll have to divide and conquer."

"Agreed," Tome acknowledged, as the team assembled around Galen's display.

"One team needs to get to Heidelberg University. The second team should stay behind to monitor the guards," Galen recommended.

Before Galen had finished his sentence, Tome reached into Galen's leather bag and pulled out two long-range walkie-talkies.

"Where did those come from?" Galen asked, surprised.

"While you were with Arden last night, I slipped into the security guards' breakroom and borrowed some equipment," Tome replied as if he had prior experience.

"That's perfect! Did you grab anything else?"

"Yes, —a slice of chocolate mousse cake," Tome admitted shamefully. "Yesterday was the curator's birthday. With no need to watch my blood sugars, I couldn't resist."

"I can stay behind to monitor the guards," Cassius offered.

"Me too," Cato echoed.

"Me three!" Cameo joined in as he snuck in from behind Galen's display. He wore his skin like a used car salesman wearing a Hawaiian shirt. Except, instead of baring curly chest hairs, he aired his breastbone. "I overheard about the mission. How exciting!"

Galen exchanged a glance of frustration with Marcel, whom he was certain had blabbed. "No one else must know about this mission. Keep a low profile," asserted Galen as he addressed the entire group.

Galen more closely inspected the two-way radios. "Since these walkie-talkies are GPS enabled, if we secure the computer from the plastination room, our progress can be tracked in real-time."

"Marcel and Tome, you'll accompany me to the university. Cato, Cassius, and Cameo, you'll monitor our progress from the jazz club storeroom. Cato, you'll oversee the maps and will guide us through the underground plexus," Galen directed.

"Roger that," Cato affirmed.

"On it! I'll snag the computer," called out Cameo.

"And grab Arden's ID badge," Galen shouted to Cameo. "Top drawer of the filing cabinet, first file." Cameo gave a thumbs up and made a beeline for the plastination room.

"Soooo, I know I look good in all my glory. I mean, look at these muscles." Marcel posed as he admired his reflection from every angle in Nila's mirror. "But we can't just walk out of here unclad. We need to disguise ourselves."

"You're right," Galen agreed. "But how?"

"We're in a museum! We can gather some clothing from the other exhibits on our way out," Marcel proposed.

"Good idea. You know the museum much better than I do. Are you certain we'll be able to find something?"

"Absolutely," Marcel reassured with a smirk. "Oh! And we need code names." Marcel was at it again with the mission impossible fantasy as he twisted the dial back and forth on the walkie-talkie.

"Put that down. We need to save the batteries," Galen urged.

"Can my code name be the *Wild Wombat*?" Marcel asked with a serious face.

"No. There will be no code names," Galen asserted. "We don't need to complicate an already challenging mission."

"We have to at least name the mission, to make it official."

"Fine," replied Galen as he gave in to Marcel's demands. "What do you want to call it?"

"Operation bosom," stated Marcel.

"Operation what?" Galen asked with a slight tilt of his head.

"B. U. S. M. - Bodies Undercover to Save Morgan," Marcel replied, just as serious as before.

"While I like acronyms, that one might not make the cut," Galen said gently, hoping to avoid explaining the obvious to Marcel.

Galen refocused the conversation by addressing the group. "To distract and detain the guards, I think we should get them a little tipsy." Galen couldn't help but recall the gas tanks he encountered in the plastination room.

"I don't think they would be keen on the *Covered Hopper*," Cassius expressed with genuine concern.

"No, not that kind of intoxication," Cato clarified. "We'll lure the guards to the plastination room and will release the curing gas. In the living, the vapors act like laughing gas and will partially sedate them. Anything the guards remember will seem like a hazy dream."

"How do you suggest we lure them to the plastination room?" Cassius asked.

Cato pondered. "The air handler sensor. The air in the plastination room must circulate continuously to prevent hazardous vapors from accumulating during fixation. If you block the vents located in each corner of the room, the sensor will send an error message to the control panel. The guards will have no choice but to check on the room."

The faint squeaking of ungreased casters diverted the group's attention. Cameo reappeared with the computer on an aluminum rolling cart and Arden's badge in hand.

"I'll block the vents," said Cassius. Invigorated by his new role, he turned to Cameo and said, "I'll need your help to reach the vents." This was no surprise as Cassius was the shortest among the group.

Marcel glanced at Arden's ID badge. "Look at that voluminous head of hair!" Marcel remarked at the feathered locks Arden fashioned in his university photo. "I wonder if his personality was as big as his hair?" Galen slipped the badge into his leather tote as the others snickered at Marcel's aspersions.

"Before you go, here. This should make you look a bit livelier." Like the pageantry of a royal coronation, Cameo presented Galen with his skin.

"Thank you, Cameo. I'll wear it proudly," Galen acknowledged, stepping into his friend's integument.

He pulled the loose skin over his face like a knitted ski mask. Galen unskillfully tightened and closed the skin along the midline of this trunk with the 3-0 silk sutures he had borrowed from the plastination room. While his persona's advanced ability to consume vast amounts of biomedical knowledge was impressive, Galen's stitching and knot-tying skills still needed more practice. "Cato, here are the university blueprints. These are too cumbersome to take with us. You'll need to guide us through the tunnel system."

"Will do," replied Cato as the exchange was made. With the blueprint canister firmly in hand, Cato left to deploy the computer in the jazz club's storeroom. Cassius and Cameo darted to the plastination room to sequester the guards.

CHAPTER 14

JENGA

Six hours, thirty minutes until crating.

Cameo and Cassius gained quick re-entry through the plastination room's unlocked door, thanks to Cameo's forward-thinking. Cassius scanned the corners of the facility for the air vents identifying four in total.

"I don't know which vent the sensor is in, so we'll need to block all of them," Cassius deduced. He contemplated how best to obstruct the airflow and scoured the room for ideas. The top filing drawer was left open from Cameo's sloppy thievery of Arden's ID badge. "These are perfect." Cassius picked up a stack of stiff empty file folders laying atop the cabinet.

Unlike Cassius's laser-like focus, the feeling of nakedness preoccupied Cameo in the absence of his skin, on loan to Galen. Across the room, Cameo leisurely inspected the tags of several grungy white lab coats hanging on a freestanding coat rack. Knowing his typical size, he first donned a large lab coat. Much to his delight, the coat was too baggy. He went down one size to a medium for a perfect fit. "I guess both cameras and skin add 10 pounds each," he said smugly.

"Cameo, give me a hand," ordered Cassius. The tails of Cameo's borrowed lab coat flared as he dashed to Cassius's aid. "If we open and hold these folders against the grates, the draw of the air into the vent should be strong enough to hold them in place."

"But we can't jump that high to place the folders," said Cameo, concerned with the logistics.

Cassius took a knee on his patella and opened the drawers on his front from his umbilicus to his clavicles. He looked like a human step stool.

"That will work!" expressed Cameo, impressed with Cassius's ingenuity.

Cameo stepped up Cassius's front. His scrawny foot displaced Cassius's black-rimmed glasses as it blindly searched for his head. As high as he could reach, Cameo strategically placed the folders to cover the majority of the vent. "Three more to go," Cameo informed as he finished covering the first vent grill.

Once they were finished, the vents resembled a bad case of shingles. Cassius twisted the valve on the curing gas canister to release the noxious fumes. Planning ahead, he rifled through the room's cabinets, gathering additional supplies. He located a spool of thick nylon cord used to suspend new specimens in their moritati poses until they cured. "Let's use this fishing line to tie the guards. And let's clean out those drainage buckets from underneath the dissection tables. We'll use them to cover the guards' heads so they can't see us."

Meanwhile, Galen, Tome, and Marcel strategized their exit in a close huddle next to Galen's display.

"Let's stop at the Ancient Greece exhibit," Marcel insisted. "My legs would look great in a toga," he rationalized.

Galen and Tome rolled their eyes as they inspected the museum's map to finalize their escape route. "Our best option is to exit through the *Underground Expedition*," said Galen, tracing his finger from the underground mine to the outdoor play yard. "We need to enter the mine on the second floor. The descending railcar will take us to the end of the exhibit on ground level. Let's get going!"

Having learned the door to the stairs was not armed, Galen ushered Tome and Marcel into the stairwell to elude the guards. Before exiting the stairwell on the second floor, the trio paused in a moment of silence. "I'll go first to make sure the hallway is clear," Galen declared. "Besides, if someone sees me, they'll think I'm a naked madman." As Galen engaged the door handle, loud muffled static interrupted his concentration.

"Chhhh… chh…chhhhhhh...Hello? Galen, come in. Do you read me? Over." The noise rang out from the walkie-talkie tucked away in Galen's bag. It was Cato.

"We hear you loud and clear," Galen replied.

"The computer is up and running. Confirm your 20." returned Cato.

"We're on the second floor in the stairwell. Over."

"Copy that," answered Cato. "The locator is working. Hold your position."

From beyond the door, the crew heard the faint signal of the sounding alarm — meep, meep, meep, meep. The annoyingly high-pitched alarm sounded like the wailing squeal of an angry armadillo.

The two guards stationed at the information kiosk near the museum's main entrance exchanged glances of confusion. The computer monitor displayed a flashing signal with an alarm code. The senior guardsman, munching on a garlic rye chip, spoke first, "I've been here for nearly 20 years. This is only the second time a sensor has ever gone off." He paused to wash down his snack with a gulp of cola. "I suppose there's a silver lining in everything. For only your second week on the job, you'll be well trained," assured the veteran.

"Which sensor is it?" asked the rookie.

"I'm not certain. We'll have to consult the manual." The senior guard pulled out a thick three-ringed binder from underneath a package of extra batteries stored in the bottom drawer of the kiosk. The rookies' patience waned as the veteran flipped one page at a time looking for the override code to quell the alarm's irritating chirp.

After six agonizingly long minutes, the guardsmen narrowed in on their search. "Based on this schematic, this sensor is in the plastination room." The senior guard continued reading. "We'll need to reset the sensor manually. There's also a handwritten note to remove the northwest vent with a Philips screwdriver. That must be where the sensor is located."

"Let's take a look. Who knew working nights at a museum could be so rousing," responded the energized rookie with a hint of sarcasm.

The guards ventured to the eighth floor. Stepping out of the elevator, the junior guard hesitated. "I have to say, this floor creeps me out a little," admitted the rookie.

"What? You don't like to walk among the dead?" egged on the veteran. "Some visitors are dying to get in here," the veteran goaded the rookie. "Keep an eye over your shoulder. Over the past couple of years, some strange unexplained things have happened on the night shift."

The rookie's eyes jerked with saccades[27] as he rapidly scanned the southeast wing for any semblance of paranormal activity. Uncertain of the senior guard's sincerity, the rookie stayed in close lockstep with his mentor as they approached the plastination room. The old guard depressed the door handle before inserting the key. "It's unlocked," he observed. "This should have been checked during rounds."

The rookie was still learning every nook and cranny of the museum. This was his first exposure to the plastination facility. The senior guard, well along in years, moseyed towards the sensor's location.

"Why are the air ducts obstructed?" the rookie inquired as he stood in the middle of the room dumbfounded by the intentionality of the placed folders.

As the senior guard peered upward to verify the

---

[27] Saccades are rapid, ballistic movements of both eyes simultaneously between fixation points.

rookie's observation, his head visibly swirled. He took a baby step backward and clumsily knelt to one knee.

"Are you okay? Are you feeling light-headed too?" expressed the rookie.

Before the veteran could turn to respond, the old man wilted to the floor.

Hearing the commotion, Cameo began to rise from his crouched position. Cassius quickly yanked on his lab coat, pulling him back to the cover of the dissection table. "One more," Cassius mouthed to Cameo while signaling the number one, pointing to the rookie.

The rookie staggered to aid his partner. Taking no more than three steps, the invisible vapors overwhelmed him. He, too, awkwardly collapsed to the floor like a wet towel.

Knowing they had to act quickly, Cameo and Cassius rushed to the guards. Working in synchronization, they maneuvered each guard to a chair. Cassius restrained the rookie's forearms behind the chair by cuffing his wrists with the heavy fishing line. As he tied the first knot, Cameo interrupted his focus.

"He keeps sliding off," Cameo whispered, referring to the senior guard's unbridled posture as he skated off the chair.

"Drape his arm over the back of the chair. It will prevent him from slumping over," recommended Cassius.

As instructed, Cameo situated the guard so that his axilla rested over the chair's back with his arm dangling behind it in the classic *Saturday night palsy*[28] position. "There," stated Cameo, pleased with his manipulation of the elder guard.

Without warning, the rookie came too. "I feel great! This is the best job ever," the young guard expressed with plastered enthusiasm while slurring his words. He raised his eyelids making eye contact with Cassius as he cinched the fishing line around the rookie's ankles.

The pure shock of Cassius's appearance made the rookie exclaim, "Wow! You look like a half-played Jenga game."

The rookie's eyelids slapped shut, and his head dropped like the slip of a bowling ball hitting the foul line. His chin came to rest on his manubrium. Cameo frettingly raised his brows as he glared at Cassius.

"You forgot the buckets," reminded Cameo.

"I know," Cassius replied, regretting his mistake. "Don't worry. When he wakes up, his bouts of awareness will seem like hallucinations." Cassius swiftly grabbed the pails and placed the tin-colored drip buckets over each guard's head.

With both guards detained, Cassius disarmed the sensor and resecured the grate. "So long as the vents are blocked, the guards will remain incapacitated. Let's get back to the storeroom to check on Cato."

As they fled to meet Cato, an iPhone caught Cameo's

---

[28] Saturday night palsy represents a compression of the radial nerve within the axilla. This compression results in wrist drop (due to muscle paralysis) and paresthesia (numbness and tingling) in the posterior arm, extensor forearm, and dorsum of the hand. Patients with this condition are unable to extend the affected wrist.

attention on the ground where the younger guard submitted to the curing gas.

"Oh…this looks interesting," Cameo said, examining the phone in wonderment. He had never operated a smartphone before, at least not that he could remember.

"Tuck it in his pocket," urged Cassius, the zealot rule follower.

"I promise I'll give it back when we come to open the vents," Cameo pleaded.

"Fine!" Cassius conceded, knowing Cameo would be relentless otherwise.

When Cameo and Cassius reached the storage room, it was apparent Cato was enjoying his role as the mission command chief. He sat reclined with his feet elevated at a makeshift desk. He stared at the computer screen that sat on the children's histology workstation. The microscopes the children looked through to appreciate human tissues were pushed to the side to accommodate the monitor. Cato's adductor pollicis muscle[29] bulged as his hand gripped a soda can. He took a noisy slurp while his eyes remained glued to the screen's stationary blinking dot.

"Are you sure you weren't an FBI operative in your past life?" Cameo asked only half-jokingly to break Cato from his trance. "Can I have a sip?"

"There's nothing like an ice-cold pop from the vend-

---

[29] The adductor pollicis muscle brings the thumb closer to the fingers to assist in gripping movements of the hand.

ing machine to keep my tissues hydrated. And the caffeine keeps my brain out of a fog," Cato stated facetiously justifying his actions. He threw back his head to finish the can. He readjusted in his chair and released a bellowing belch.

Cameo and Cassius exchanged glances of amusement. Neither had ever seen this relaxed side of Cato before. He'd always seemed so uptight and poised.

"Excuse me! Okay, back to business. Are the guards secure?"

"Affirmative," Cassius replied. "They won't be doing rounds anytime soon."

Cato raised the walkie-talkie to the genu of his mandible and called over the airwaves, "All clear! I repeat, all clear!"

CHAPTER 15

Five hours until crating.

Galen, Marcel, and Tome rushed through the stairwell door and raced across the second-floor vestibule with an increased sense of urgency. As they passed the *Secrets of the Samurai* exhibit, Marcel slowed his pace to shop for a disguise. With all his might, he pried at the decorative sixteenth-century Karuta armor fitted to a mannequin's torso. The Samurai warrior's armor remained securely fastened to its post, just as the museum curators had intended, due to its value.

"We don't have time for this!" Tome urged in a winded voice as he raced back to grab Marcel, who reluctantly abandoned the flashy armored sheath.

The three, now reunited, picked up their stride. They rounded a corner of the great hall guarded by an ornate bronze cannon recovered from a Spanish galleon. The hallway, the length of two tennis courts, ended at the entrance to the *Underground Expedition*. Half the distance to the entrance, Vitalis sprung out like a spooky jack-in-the-box toy with his trusty ostrich in tow. Aside from the felt amber hat he wore to cover his empty cranium, Vitalis resembled Hermes, the messenger of the Olympic gods, wrapped in a Greek tunic. To the team's amazement, an assorted wardrobe draped the base of the ostrich's neck.

Galen glared at Marcel like a lion ready to devour its prey.

"What?" Marcel replied with a shrug of his shoulders. "This is the most excitement we've had in years," he justified. "I may have let the plan slip a time or two."

Vitalis unfolded the disguises one by one to present each with their outfit.

"A toga!" expressed Marcel with delight. Vitalis winked.

Next, Vitalis dressed Tome in a tight black and white fitted shirt. The shirt's horizontal stripes nicely complimented his axial cross-sections. The black cotton pants Tome squeezed into looked more like capris with the hem ending mid-shank. To complete the ensemble, Vitalis slung red suspenders over Tome's shoulders and fastened them to his pants.

"What am I supposed to be?" Tome inquired.

"A mime, of course! That reminds me. I grabbed this from the *Revenge of the Pharaohs* exhibit." Vitalis revealed a small alabaster jar of white steel pigment. "Rub this on your face," he ordered. Vitalis handed a second jar of chestnut-colored dye to Marcel to help mask the fiber striations of his exposed musculature. Lastly, Vitalis presented Galen with his attire, which he begrudgingly received.

"Lederhosen made you think of me?" Galen queried, a bit perplexed. "I'm flattered," he responded from the corner of his mouth.

Marcel snickered, hardly containing himself. "In that getup, your code name should be *Hunky Hans*," he bantered.

"For the last time, there will be no code names," Galen grunted, regretting not having assigned Marcel to Cato's team.

"Here, put on this hat," said Vitalis as he removed the felt alpine hat from atop his brainless skull. "It will bring out the russet irises of your eyes," he remarked.

"I hope we don't look too conspicuous," Galen voiced with a touch of uncertainty as the amateur fashionista distributed apt footwear.

"Oh, and here. Take these with you in case you run into any trouble," said Vitalis. He deposited a handful of Egyptian gold coins into Galen's hand.

Galen gave a polite nod and stowed the coins in the inner recess of his leather tote. "Thanks, Vitalis," he said, hoping the remainder of the mission would bring far fewer surprises. "Back to the task at hand," Galen commanded. "We need to get to the play yard."

At the *Underground Expedition*, they walked between the stanchions and velvet ropes toward the mineshaft's sloped elevator rails. With each step, the exhibit grew darker and darker.

"Maybe we should have taken the stairs," suggested

Tome.

"This is the closest exit to the bus stop," reminded Galen, before Marcel interjected his two cents.

"Going through the *Hall of Gems* is the only other way to reach this exit. But every night, it's closed up tighter than a camel's anal sphincter in a sandstorm," added Marcel, unable to resist the extra imagery.

"Aren't there any emergency lights in this place? I can't see a thing," Tome muttered. He blindly searched in an erratic pattern for any semblance of a landmark.

"You would think a mine like this would have lamps or something..., OUCH!" Galen yelped as he rammed his hip's anterior superior iliac spine[30] into the cantilevered corner of a square stationary mass. With an outstretched hand, Galen patted down the object in question. It was undoubtedly the mining car, he deduced. Keeping one hand on the mining car, Galen reached blindly for Tome until he located his forearm. "Tome, hop in while Marcel and I find the control panel to start the lift. It must be nearby."

Marcel's sandaled feet stumbled over the iron rails as he walked about the periphery of the mining car. "Too bad the guards didn't have any night vision goggles. Those would be handy right now. Tome, why didn't you score a flashlight from the breakroom? Wait, let me guess — the chocolate mousse distracted you."

"I'm glad it's dark in here. Your face is much more

---

[30] The anterior superior iliac spine (ASIS) is a bony landmark of the pelvis that represents the anterior termination of the iliac crest (the ridge felt when placing one's hands on the hips).

tolerable this way," Tome jabbed back.

"Gentlemen, we're not here to roast each other! Focus."

Marcel went for the uppercut, "Yeah, well at least I can hold myself together. You're such an insecure pansy, you'd dump your girlfriend for a date with...."

"Eureka!" Galen exclaimed as he flipped a lever mounted to the fake stone wall. A series of hanging lanterns illuminated one by one dimly lighting the depths of the sloping mineshaft.

Nearby sat a conventional control panel for the rail conveyor system. A large green pushbutton labeled *ON* occupied the center of the console. Marcel's fist reflexively struck the green doodad like a four-year-old boy wanting to activate anything with a button. The rail conveyor roared to life with a chattering rumble. The mining car jolted so abruptly it displaced Tome's slices from his head to his cervical spine.

"Hurry! Hop in," called Tome as he reoriented his face. Tome extended his hand to help Marcel into the car. When Marcel grabbed hold, Tome's wrist sections disarticulated from his forearm. Tome gave Marcel a crooked smile. Marcel caught himself as he stumbled. He chucked the slices at Tome's head as he vaulted into the mine car. Galen, holding his hat to his head with one hand and his tote in the other, chased in pursuit. He tossed in his bag and jumped aboard.

As they coasted past the first spiraling turn, Galen called into the storeroom, "Cato. We're on the move.

Ahead is a "Y" in the track. Do we go left or right?"

"Bear right. It will take you to the railcar repair dock. Look for an illuminated exit sign. It will lead you straight to the playground," Cato advised.

"We have to switch the track!" Tome observed. "Heading left will take us to the exhibit."

The narrow mineshaft left no room on either side of the railcar. Running on the rails ahead of the mining car to engage the switch seemed too precarious. The track's switch lever rested at an oblique angle, just out of reach, eight yards ahead.

In search of a solution to pull the track lever vertically, Tome unclasped his suspenders. He held the suspender clips in both hands forming a loop. As he leaned outstretched over the edge of the railcar, his slices shifted one atop the other. Like a novice expanding an accordion, the extra extension was all he needed. Tome lobbed the loop of suspenders around the switch lever and yanked with more force than he needed to. He's lucky the elastic bands held together. The track ahead clacked into place as it changed course.

Marcel, only mildly impressed with Tome's quick thinking, paid him a backhanded compliment, "Not bad for an unstable pile of sliced entrails." Before Marcel could admire the look on Tome's face, the lights lining the shaft suddenly went dark.

Back in the storeroom, Cato expressed outrage. The monitor was unresponsive, and the storeroom was pitch-black. "A power outage at a time like this? What are the chances?" Cato bemoaned.

In the mineshaft, the wheels screeched as the persistent hum of the rail conveyer ceased. The railcar coasted to a halt.

"This blackout reminds me of the time Vitalis tried to hot wire the neon *Dead End* sign over the alleyway between the jazz club and Mr. Camper's bakery," Marcel reminisced. "Come to think of it, the jolt of electricity he received that night does explain a lot."

"Cato, do you read me?"

"I read you, Galen. There's been a power outage. I'm going to reset the breaker in the subbasement."

"I guess we'll have to walk from here," Galen surmised. "Everyone out. Follow the tracks to the right. And watch your step," he cautioned.

Huddled together, the three continued on foot through the seemingly endless tunnel. They crept gingerly through the darkness until Galen noticed a red radiating speck in the distance. "There's the exit," he said, alerting the others.

With a marker in sight, the trio picked up their pace. The red glow grew larger and came into clearer focus as the exit drew near. Several feet from the egress, the regularity of the evenly spaced rail ties beneath their feet ended and transitioned to the smooth concrete floor of the repair dock.

Galen thrust open the exit door. He immediately felt the breeze of the evening's crisp summer air. It reminded him of the walks to the library he would take with Morgan. The moonlit sky illuminated the empty playground in front of them. They heard only the noise of the wind rustling the trees beyond the yard's black iron fence.

"I think that's the bus stop," Tome said, straining his eyes at the distant corner.

"We need bus 321," Galen reminded the team.

The trio hurried across the playground and exited the yard through a side gait in the wrought iron fence. Parading down the sidewalk, their shadows appeared and faded as they passed under the evenly spaced lampposts.

In front of the bus stop, a group of fraternity brothers rolled to a stop in a carmine red Porsche convertible. Its beaming headlamps spotlighted the trio in the crosswalk. One of the backseat passengers yelled out, "Hey lunatics, the society of freaks and nut jobs called, and they want their wardrobe back!"

"Your ignorance makes the ocean look like a puddle," Galen retorted in his mind while pelting the heckler with a look of glaring disdain. The driver forcefully revved the engine. Galen's new, more mature, persona wasn't nearly as spontaneous or punchy as his former youthful temperament. The frat brothers mocked Galen with flapping mouths.

Tome, realizing the ineffectiveness of Galen's searing scowl, took matters into his own hands. Without thought, Tome made a gruesome face. With his hands, he expanded his head releasing each of his slices in succession like a dealer doing a waterfall card flourish.

"Go, go, go!" exclaimed the astounded antagonizing passenger.

Marcel locked his eyes on the Porsche as it sped off. He raised a clenched hand extending a fist bump to Tome. Tome reciprocated. Galen was none the wiser to the events behind him.

The three studied a weathered transportation route posted on the panel of the overhanging bus shelter. They interpreted their location as being seven stops from the university. Galen restlessly shifted his weight from one foot to the other. "Now, we wait."

CHAPTER 16

INCOGNITO

B us 321 arrived barreling into the stop. The folding doors sprung open well before the bus came to an abrupt whiplashing halt. The driver overshot the bus stop by at least ten feet.

"It's a busy night. There's no time to waste. Hop on," shouted a rotund woman from the driver's seat. Her voice had enough gravel in it to pave a driveway.

"Maybe we should walk," Tome objected, skeptical of their safety.

"It will be fine. You heard the woman. There is no time to waste," Galen prodded with renewed enthusiasm as he shoved Tome aboard. "This is our only chance to save Morgan, so tighten your suspenders and find a little courage."

Galen charged up the steps behind Tome. The bus driver's embroidered name patch read, *Gertrude.* Tome felt her name perfectly matched her overt rudeness. Galen attempted to deposit the Egyptian coin into the pay meter, but it was too thick for the coin slot. Recognizing the uniqueness of the gold coin, the bus driver extended her hand to receive it. She raised her cat eye shaped glasses to closely inspect the artifact. The authentic coin's density and embossed inscriptions were uniquely convincing. She waved the three on through and tucked the coin securely in her top pocket.

As Galen looked down the aisle to take a seat, he was astonished by what he saw. Passengers crowded the bus, each dressed in a costume.

"I think we'll fit in just fine," whispered Marcel to Galen.

No seats were available. It was standing room only. Galen, Marcel, and Tome stood incognito between a young teenage girl dressed as a pink elephant and an older gentleman who fashioned a jester's costume. Two seats away from where they stood, Marcel spotted a woman dressed as a Raggedy Ann doll reading an advertisement. The cover read, *Carnival in Cologne*.

"Look up," Galen whispered, nudging Marcel in an intercostal space. Colorful billboards marketing the carnival decorated the bus's canopy. *Carnival in Cologne: A time of merrymaking in the streets!*

"Excuse me," said a man dressed in a skeleton suit as he rose from his seat and proceeded to the exit doors.

"Can you believe that? Since when do humans only have eight ribs on each side? And the vertebral column is totally off," Tome grumbled to Galen and Marcel with an absolute aversion to inaccuracies. "Ivory would be appalled!"

"And look at who he's with," returned Marcel. The three directed their attention to a man whose costume included hand-painted muscles on a nude-colored spandex bodysuit. "That guy wishes his biceps were that big," remarked Marcel. "I think he was a tad over-zealous with the paintbrush."

"Train stop for connection to the carnival," announced the bus driver in her grungy monotone voice over the distorted intercom.

Again, the doors flung open before the bus recoiled to a stop. The trio remained stationary as the carnival-goers swirled past them, fleeing to the sidewalk in one mass exodus. Some shared a brief look of disgust as they caught a whiff of Galen's freshly plastinated aroma. Now, only the trio occupied the bus.

"Are you getting off?" questioned the driver as she glared at the three in the oversized rearview mirror.

Galen's head swiveled as he indicated, no. The driver, a bit perplexed, recalled the gold coin tucked safely in her pocket. She tipped her head, giving them the benefit of the doubt. Her piercing stare put Galen on edge. "University, next stop," the driver said as she released her foot from the brake pedal and sealed the doors.

The trio took a momentary pause to survey their surroundings as they stepped from the bus onto the sidewalk. Though it was dark, they could appreciate the university's regal academic buildings surrounded by impeccably maintained landscapes. Only two students could be seen sauntering through the courtyards amid the dated school buildings as the night's tepid midsummer air swept through the stone-lined corridors.

"Galen, where do we go from here?" Tome asked.

"We need the sidewalk behind the Molecular Biology building. It's over here to the right." Galen passed the walkie-talkie to Tome. "Update Cato on our progress," Galen suggested as he strolled in the direction of the access point.

"Cato, do you read me?" Tome called over the two-way radio.

"Cato is still in the subbasement working on the power outage," Cassius replied.

Galen intervened, reclaiming the device from Tome. "We're about to enter the tunnel system. You have the university schematics. You'll need to guide us through. Over."

"Roger that!" Cameo and Cassius said in unison, pleased with their synchronization.

The tunnel access point was an unassuming grate level with the surrounding sidewalk but adjacent to the main pathway. The spaces between the grate's steal gridlines were no larger than paper currency. A gust of wind kicked up, displacing small clumps of cottonwood fluff overtop of the metal grating.

Marcel and Galen peered through the grate while Tome stood guard. "I see the release lever," announced Marcel. "Hand me the nylon line."

Galen passed Marcel a single six-foot strand of fishing line from his tote. "Make a slip knot before you lower it."

Marcel made quick work of the slip knot and threaded the line between the metal lattices. He carefully lowered the line to the level of the release mechanism.

"That's it," encouraged Galen. "Steady. Give it a little swing and loop the lever."

The line effortlessly encircled the lever, like a groom sliding a wedding band on his bride's finger. Marcel lightly tugged on the line to synch the loop around the release arm. He stood up and wrapped the line twice around both hands. Marcel yanked on the line like wrenching the pull string of a two-stroke engine. The fishing line immediately snapped in two. All, except a foot of line, fell to the tunnel's floor.

"Oh boy!" muttered Marcel.

"Marcel! Are you kidding me?" exclaimed Galen. "We have no more fishing line and now it's too short to reach the lever." Galen internally scolded himself again for not assigning Marcel to Cato's team.

"I'm sorry, Galen. That's what you get when a tugboat pulls a barge with a parachute cord," joked Marcel, suggesting his brute strength was no match for the inadequate fishing line. "Now what? Not to state the obvious but asking for an escort to the cadaver lab from the security office doesn't seem like a viable option."

"We need to figure out something. Standing idle is never a solution." The distress in Galen's voice was palpable.

Tome took a seat on a nearby slatted bench to strategize. As he lowered his weight to the bench, half of his buttock slices slipped through the bench's fissures like dropping bread into a toaster.

"This mission is falling apart," Marcel scoffed. "Just look at Tome, he can hardly keep himself together." Marcel paced down the sidewalk. "Maybe we could ram that glass window with this trash canister to slip inside." Marcel pointed at a double-hung window reachable with the aid of the bench. His suggestion came as no surprise to Tome. Marcel was the type who would use any excuse to break something.

"No, we're not going to damage any property," Galen retorted, killing Marcel's enthusiasm. As the youngest member of the group, counted in both lived and death years, Galen never anticipated having to be the mature voice of reason.

"So that means we can't pry the window open with that flagpole either?" suggested Tome in the form of a cautious question.

Across the paved street along the river's bank, stood a solitary bronze flagpole. The pole, no taller than an upright man on a bicycle, leaned at a slight angle, just enough to see the striped flag's unmistakable Heidelberg University insignia. The crowds from the regatta's festivities left the river's embankments littered with miscellaneous assortments of odds and ends, including the makeshift flagpole.

"That's it. I have an idea," asserted Galen with renewed fervor. Galen forcibly jerked the flagpole from side to side to loosen it from the earth's grip. He returned jogging from across the street. The flag flew over his shoulder like an Olympian taking a victory lap. He knelt beside his leather tote and pulled out a pair of dissection scissors. He quickly detached the flag from the bronze-colored pole and cut the wool into three half-inch-wide strips along the flag's length. He tied all three strips together with a knot on one end and motioned Marcel to hold the knot tight. He proceeded to braid the strips into a single cloth rope no longer than the width of the flag.

"This is even shorter than the fishing line we have left," expressed Marcel. "How is this going to help?"

Galen ignored Marcel's question, in part because of his focused concentration but mostly because he did not feel compelled to address the peanut gallery. Galen finished what looked like a child's arts and crafts project and refastened the braided cloth rope to the bronze flagpole after tying a slip knot.

"There!" Galen exclaimed proud of his makeshift work. The apparatus looked like a useless miniature dog-catching noose. Without hesitation, he lowered the device through the grate's openings past the release arm. He gingerly swung and raised the pole to loop and tighten the noose around the lever. "I've got it. Here goes nothing."

Galen repositioned his grip and pulled on the inverted flagpole like he was wrestling the roots of an unwanted sapling out of the ground. Marcel side-stepped to hide behind Tome when he heard the extra strain placed on the braided rope. Just to annoy Marcel, Tome slid his entire upper body to the right so that only his pelvis and lower limbs shielded Marcel. Suddenly, the grate let out an abrupt moan as it gave way with a sharp spring-like release.

"Great work team! I knew we could do it," praised Marcel who contributed very little. "Next stop, the cadaver lab."

CHAPTER 17

PAC-MAN

Four hours, forty-five minutes until crating.

"We're in the tunnel," Galen called to the command center. "Be ready to provide directions once we reach the first junction." The airwaves remained silent. No reply. "Let's move ahead."

The tunnel plexus was surprisingly well-lit. The damp air smelled stale and musty, like the cover of an old leather-bound book. It was clear the bare concrete walls were made for fortification. A series of cast iron pipes of varying sizes hung by metal straps ran neatly along the crease where the wall and ceiling met. As far as the three could see and hear, only they occupied the tunnel. Eventually, the team's demeanor relaxed. Marcel grew more eager to meet their fellow kind.

"Arden mentioned the medical center acts as the central node where all the tunnels converge. There is a direct connection between the Medical Sciences building and the hospital. That's how they transport the corpses between the morgue and the anatomy lab," Galen explained as the team kept a steady but cautious pace. "From what I recall on the blueprints, the route to the

Medical Sciences building is at the second right."

As they approached the first confluence of intersecting tunnels, Cassius's voice came over the device. "Right! Right! Come on. Quickly!"

Tome, Marcel, and Galen exchanged looks of confusion. "I thought you said the second right," Marcel stressed.

"That's a good move! It will get you to our goal more quickly," said Cassius with audible confidence.

"They do have us on GPS and are referencing the blueprints directly," Tome pointed out.

Galen, succumbing to Cassius's suggestion, turned down the hallway at the first right.

"Now left. Then right. Then right again," Cassius rattled off.

"Slow down. We can't keep up!" responded Galen in a quickened breath over the radio.

"Wait! No! Nooooooooo! So close," Cameo bemoaned.

"What is going on? You two need to work together," Galen snapped into the walkie-talkie. "Which direction is it?"

"PAC-MAN is so addicting," expressed Cameo faintly in the background. "Even without my past memories, I'm betting this was one of my childhood favorites."

Galen exhaled an audible growl of frustration. "Cassius! Cameo!" He yelled into the device, gripping it tight enough to crush it.

"Are you talking to us?" Cameo responded from the other end.

"No, I'm talking to my late aunt Eugenia. Yes! Of course, I'm talking to you," Galen lashed out. "What are you doing?"

"We thought you would page us when you needed our help. We're playing some games on the guard's smartphone I snagged." Cameo shamefully admitted.

"Where is Cato?" inquired Galen.

"The power is still off. We're waiting for him to return," Cassius answered.

"Listen to me carefully." Galen's blood pressure would have been off the charts if he had blood and a pumping heart. "Turn on the phone's flashlight. Next, unroll the blueprints and find the tunnel schematic." Galen paused, allowing time for Cassius and Cameo to follow his lead.

"We have the schematic," replied Cameo.

"Find the Molecular Biology building and trace the route to the first right, followed by a left. Now, go right twice more."

"Okay. Now, what?" responded Cassius.

"Your finger should be on our current location. Where are we?" asked Galen.

"You're next to the animal research facility."

"That explains the smell," Marcel chimed in. "I thought Tome had the vapors."

"Moving forward, I need you to focus on *our* maze,"

Galen huffed stressing his discontent, "not the game. We can't afford any more distractions." Understanding the source of Galen's frustration, Tome and Marcel laid low realizing the need to mute their opinions.

"The power is on," announced Cassius. "We have your GPS on the screen now. Turn back from the way you came," Cassius instructed, hoping to recalibrate the team from their unintended setback. Following Cassius's every instruction, the trio arrived at an oversized freight elevator. The signage above the dull, dusty doors read *Medical Sciences*.

"This must be it!" Tome cheered as he pressed the button to summon the lift. The doors peeled open. The three jockeyed for a position inside.

"The lab is adjacent to the elevator," Galen explained, pressing his digitus secundus[31] on the button labeled 4. He couldn't help but feel on edge, realizing they were gradually making their way closer to Morgan. With so many variables yet to overcome, he could only prepare for one step at a time.

Within seconds, the doors sprung open. Galen marched out of the elevator taking the lead. To the right, an inset doorway labeled with a placard read, *Anatomy Laboratory*.

"Oh, man! We did it!" Marcel squealed with excitement.

"This is just the beginning," Galen said in a calm and collected voice.

---

[31] The term digitus secundus is Latin for second digit, the index finger. The first digit is the thumb.

A tiny red light on the door's card reader signaled the door was secure. Galen retrieved Arden's badge and waved it across the sensor. The red indicator light persisted.

"Arden has been dead for at least three years. I'm not too surprised his badge isn't registering," rationalized Tome.

"Try it again," urged Marcel. Galen touched the card to the reader again, this time in slow motion.

No beep. Not even a flicker. It meant only one thing. The department had deactivated Arden's badge. Deflated, Marcel slid to a seated position; his back pressed against the wall. "Now what?" asked Marcel. "This place is sealed tighter than a dolphin's blow hole. I doubt knocking on the door will rouse the dead."

Feeling it was worth a shot in the dark, Galen rapped on the door three times. No response. Like a confident male at a girl's sweet sixteen pool party, Tome undressed dropping his shirt on Marcel's head.

"What are you doing, exactly?" asked Marcel. "There is no way you can pick this lock with your suspenders. Even Galen's medical instruments are no match for this door," Marcel lamented.

Tome, now looking more like his usual self, struck his heel against the floor in a backward sweeping motion. The slices of his foot spread apart like loose pages in a ream of paper. One at a time, Tome slid each of his slices under the door. "Give me a hand," Tome insisted.

Finally appreciating Tome's plan, Marcel and Galen

disarticulated Tome one piece at a time and slipped him through the half-inch crack between the base of the door and the linoleum floor. On the other side of the door, Tome reassembled himself from his feet to his torso. Like a headless horseman, Tome's reconnected parts searched blindly for the door handle to no avail. Not knowing how the cadavers on the other side might receive Tome, Galen and Marcel held their breath, hoping he would pull through as they passed the dome of his calvarium under the lab's entryway. After reattaching his neck and head, Tome finally located the handle. The door swung open. Tome was a hot mess with many disheveled and misplaced slices. It looked like a first grader had pieced him together. Marcel and Galen quickly reshuffled Tome and returned his mime disguise.

The cadaver lab was cold and dim. The moonlight shining through the top windows revealed row upon row of cadaver tanks in the shadows. To the living, unaccustomed to such a space, the facility emanated an uncanny vibe. The trio, however, felt at ease, confident in what they might expect.

"Let's add some light to the subject," Marcel remarked, flipping on a light switch just inside the doorway. In the blink of an eye, the fluorescent lights illuminated the room with a sterile brightness. Galen couldn't help but squint as his sphincter pupillae muscles[32] constricted to abate the influx of light. Graphite-colored

---

[32] The autonomic nervous system controls the size of the pupils by stimulating one of two muscles in the iris of the eye. The sympathetic, 'fight-or-flight', division of the autonomic nervous system controls the dilator pupillae muscle which opens the pupil to allow more light into the eye. Conversely,

chalkboards lined the periphery of the room. The speckled French gray epoxy floors clashed with the drab stainless steel tanks. The air reeked of pungent formaldehyde.

Tome casually turned to view the wall adjacent to the door where they had entered. A poem titled, "Our Fallen Teacher," written by a former medical student was inscribed on the wall in an elegant long flowing script.

Tome read the last two stanzas aloud.

> *"I have come where the dead*
> *Mingle with the living*
> *And the fallen teach*
> *To the future giving.*
> *I am your fallen teacher."*

Uninspired by the poem's symbolism, Marcel shrugged off Tome like a preoccupied child leaping between floor tiles at a fine art museum. "What now?"

Just then, the team heard a faint creaking noise from the far corner of the room.

"Who's there?" Marcel shuttered, adjusting his posture to ready himself for action.

Galen meandered across the room between the tanks toward the clatter's origin. Convinced he was in the right location, Galen flung the clamshell lids of one tank wide open. The deafening clangor of the aluminum lids striking the metal leg posts was intense enough to wake

---

the parasympathetic, 'rest and digest', division causes the pupil's diameter to decrease by activating the sphincter pupillae muscle.

the dead, though it didn't. Galen stood over the head of an undraped body. The disposition of the cadaver was not at all what Galen had expected. A quick full-body scan revealed a torn brachial plexus and an opened chest cavity showing a lung inflicted with saw gouges. The specimen's infratemporal fossa looked as though it was dissected with a cheese grater.

"Hellooooo," Galen called in sing-song vibrato. The body lay unresponsive. "It's ok. We're friends of a friend." No response. Festering up the fading memories of his debating skills, Galen tried to arouse the body from a legal angle. "The Code of Silence only forbids you to speak directly to the living. Communication among our kind is permissible." Still nothing. Grasping at straws, Galen goaded the cadaver hoping to provoke him. "Your moritati pose is uniquely haphazard."

"We stiffen in the posture our students leave us in," the less-than-pristine specimen uttered, offended by Galen's rude remark. "Given you know of the Code of Silence and the moritati pose, you must be legit," the specimen rationalized, keeping his upside-down gape fixed on Galen. "Who are you, exactly?"

"My name is Galen, and we are here in need of your help. What's your name?" Marcel and Tome glanced over Galen's shoulder to put a face with the voice.

"My students call me Maurice," stated the tattered specimen as he sat up erect on the tabletop. He moved so swiftly that his skullcap slid from his head onto the table. "So, you need OUR help? Why ever would such meticulously kept specimens, like yourselves, need help from us?" Maurice inquired as if the popular kids were genuinely asking for help from a high school science team of misfits.

"I need to access Simon Floundary's office. Arden mentioned you would have the information I need to help my...friend," Galen explained.

"He's incapable of saying the word girlfriend." Marcel felt Galen's sidestepping pause needed clarification. "You could call her your playmate. Then you wouldn't have to say girlfriend," Marcel rationalized in only a way that he could.

"Arden?!" chimed in a voice from across the room. "We all have great respect for Arden." The trio turned around to see another specimen climbing down off a distant stainless steel slab. A crisp white sheet wrapped her torso like a strapless dress. Whoever had dissected her had skipped a section in Grant's Dissector in preparation for the forearm lab. Nearly every tendon in her flexor forearm hung unattached. Though she was clearly in better shape than Maurice, she held her mangled forearm at her side so as not to attract attention to it. "My name is Gloria." She looked aimlessly around the room. "Folks, wake up! We have visitors," she announced as she pounded her fist on a nearby tank, waking the slumbering cadavers. Within moments, the room surged to life.

Gloria sported a shaved head. A visible butterfly tattoo marked the remaining skin overlying her ankle's lateral malleolus.[33] Gloria's demeanor appeared rough around the edges, like a strong woman warrior. For Marcel, it was love at first sight. He instinctively fluttered his winged pecs. His reflected pectoralis major muscles[34] popped out from beneath his toga as if engaging in a customary mating ritual. Gloria returned an unexpected wink in Marcel's direction.

"Marcel, put your pecs away," muttered Tome from the corner of his mouth. "You know better. The Code of Celibacy forbids any romantic relationships." Under the Code of Celibacy, bodies were expected to refrain from courtships. Despite it being physically impossible for dead bodies to biologically procreate, the Council of Corpses sought to establish a certain level of sophistication and purity in the realm, for all cadavers, not just plastinates.

"I'm dying to ask, wherever did you get that tunic?" Maurice inquired of Marcel to veer the conversation away from Tome's scolding.

"Isn't it great?" Marcel blurted as he dazzled everyone with his charisma. He turned from side to side to give Maurice the full effect.

Galen tensed and his discontented mood intensified. "Enough about that, Marcel. Maurice, can you tell me about Simon Floundary's office, and more importantly,

---

[33] The distal end of the fibula flares to form the lateral malleolus; the prominent bump felt on the outer ankle.
[34] The pectoralis major muscles cover most of the front of the chest and act on the humerus by flexing, adducting (bringing the arm down to the side of the body), and medially (internally) rotating the arm at the shoulder joint.

how I can access it?"

"It's on the second floor. Why do you ask?" Gloria questioned.

"My best friend's life depends on it. Her health is deteriorating. Starting her on Dr. Floundary's new drug trial will practically cure her and will add years of longevity to her life," Galen gushed. "While living, I was an invisible nobody and powerless. There was nothing I could do to improve her health or well-being. But now, I know Simon's research will save her. She deserves the best care possible. I'll do anything to help her. I have to try."

"You certainly are devoted and have a caring heart," expressed Gloria. "I'm sorry to hear about your friend's condition. What's her name?" she asked, hoping her empathy would provide Galen with a morsel of comfort.

"M-, M-," Galen paused, unable to say her name.

"Morgan," Marcel jumped in. "Her name is Morgan."

"It's starting!" Tome whispered to Marcel. "It's only a matter of hours now," Tome stated referring to the final stages of Galen's transformation. "If we don't hurry, Morgan will be dismissed from his mind, and he'll fail to remember why we're even on this mission."

"That sounds serious." Gloria acknowledged, overhearing the strain in Tome's voice.

"While we would love to rehash how we got here, we, unfortunately, don't have the time," Marcel announced in an urgent tone. Long story short, Galen's transformation is starting to take hold, and if he forgets who his girlfriend is before he reaches her, more than just memories could be lost. Gloria, my dear, can you help Galen get into Dr. Simon Floundary's office?"

"You may have noticed the lab is secured with a badge reader, unlike the other rooms and offices in the building. Because of the lab's keycard access, Ted, the department's IT specialist, keeps a hide-a-key box in the back prep room with a master skeleton key. On more than one occasion, Ted has used it to access his own office. If his head weren't attached, he would misplace it too," Gloria assured. "Open the top center cabinet. The matchstick-sized box is secured magnetically under the lip of the bottom shelf."

Galen methodically waded through the prep room where spare tanks and surgical equipment obstructed his path to the cabinets flanking the west wall. Like a sliding puzzle game, he moved three empty cadaver tanks, a c-arm, and a laparoscopy tower to clear a walkway. The master brass key was exactly where Gloria said it was. Galen knew Arden's instincts were right. The medical school cadavers were valuable allies.

Galen emerged from the pit of the disheveled prep room tightly clenching the key in his palm. Gloria, now sitting leisurely with legs crossed on the edge of a tank continued, "Once you are in Simon's office, there is a single inner door that leads to his neighboring lab space. He always keeps that door unlocked. A white drug safe on the lab's benchtop contains the vials of Ribozore you're looking for," Gloria added, inferring Galen's intent without him ever mentioning the medication.

"How did you know I was after Ribozore?"

"We are the custodians of new and undiscovered biomedical knowledge for our university. We know every researcher and every research study they have ever performed. We're the ones who released the knowledge of Ribozore to Simon and his research team." Marcel drooled over Gloria's intellect and devotion to her duties. "You'll also need the code to access the subject database if you expect Morgan to receive multiple rounds of therapy."

Galen scanned the room for something to write on. He located a plastic wall-mounted brochure holder with a stack of pamphlets. Paying no attention to the advertisement, Galen swiped a single flyer. He snatched a blue ballpoint pen from a Mayo stand adjacent to the lab's eyewash station. "I'm ready. What's the password?"

"J, E, S, S, E, - all caps - 5, 1, 2, - no spaces," Gloria spelled out. "His office number is 206."

"Thank you. You may have just saved a life," Galen expressed with visible gratitude. "Let's go!" Galen called to Marcel and Tome with renewed hope as he darted to leave.

"Hold up!" Marcel shouted. "We don't get to meet others like us very often. I've never met a cadaver before that has not been plastinated. Maybe Tome and I should stay behind to get to know these specimens a little better. And maybe Gloria can help us find some scrubs, so we don't raise suspicion at the hospital." Surprisingly, Marcel stated a convincing case, though Galen suspected his real intention was to spend more time with Gloria.

"Alright," Galen agreed, somewhat reluctantly. "I'll meet you back here in 30 minutes or less. Don't cause a ruckus while I'm gone. Keep a low profile," he warned sternly.

As Galen left the cadaver lab, Tome chastised Marcel. "He shouldn't go alone. What if his memory fades quicker than most? He could become disoriented and wander off."

Preoccupied with charming Gloria, Marcel brushed off Tome's concern for Galen. "He'll be fine."

CHAPTER 18

THE CUPBOARD

G alen swiftly descended the stairwell en route to Simon's office. He imagined Simon as a brilliant intellectual scientist with a worry-free life and a deep devotion to his groundbreaking research. In truth, Simon was quite ordinary and had just as many flaws as most other academics. Like many, Simon struggled to balance his family life with his work life. The priorities of work all too often interfered with dinner table conversations, special events, and even vacations.

Feeling a swell of excitement, Galen slid down the lower half of the handrail leading to the second-floor exit. "200... 202... 204," he counted as his enthusiasm escalated. Knowing he was so close to changing Morgan's life for the better, his sympathetic nervous system's fight-or-flight response kicked into hyperdrive as he inserted the key to unlock the door.

The quaint office was as dark as a cavernous sinus and felt like the drafty entrance of a cave. The whooshing sound of a wobbly ceiling fan hummed in time with an oscillating rhythmic tick. Reaching blindly around the corner of the doorframe, Galen flipped on the lights. The desk and bookcases were surprisingly neat and tidy. Colored prints of unidentifiable microscopic tissues hung on the walls. Galen got the impression Simon might not fit the stereotypical mold of a disheveled professor.

The inner door Gloria had described was left wide open as if inviting Galen into the space. Stepping across the threshold felt like passing into an inner sanctum. The laboratory was nearly quadruple the size of Simon's office. Three separate bays of workstations were separated by cotton-white storage cabinets beneath black-speckled countertops with a pearl finish. Open shelving above the countertops formed partial partitions between the bays. Along the left-hand side of the first aisle, rows of bottled chemicals and compounds lined the wall alphabetically. A narrow wooden door tucked itself between the end of the compounds and the rear windows overlooking an administrative building. The slim width and position of the door led Galen to assume it was a storage closet.

The drug safe sat perched on the workbench in the back-right corner of the first bay. Much to Galen's surprise, the *drug safe* was nothing more than a dingy white cabinet made of cheap composite materials. He unfastened the medicine cupboard's hook-shaped latch to reveal five rows of tiny glass vials sealed with crimped aluminum caps. The label's print was so small, he held the vial inches from his face to read, "Ribozore, 75 mcg per ml." Galen exhaled as he grasped the vial tightly in his hand as if wrapping his arms around Morgan.

Instinctively, Galen returned the cupboard to its original state, minus one vial. With elation, he skated back to the office and sat down at Simon's computer. Galen pulled the pamphlet from his lederhosen's back pocket and placed it on the desk. He shook the mouse like a drug addict in withdrawal. The monitor illuminated, and the password screen appeared. Galen entered the password characters pecking one key at a time. The computer unlocked revealing an open database. The repository of enlisted subjects was extensive. The database contained an archived history of every subject Simon had ever contacted throughout his many years as a translational researcher. Scrolling down the alphabetical list of trial participants, Galen jumped to the Ls. "Please be in here. Please," Galen begged as he read through the last names. Lombardy, Loskoff, Loughlin, Lubeck. There was no entry for Morgan Lowe. Out of desperation, Galen proceeded to enter Morgan's information into the form that populated the database. With his eyes focused mostly on the keyboard, he typed out her first name until his concentration was interrupted by the ding of the elevator beyond the door. Galen's mind raced in a frenzy like a frightened wild animal trying to escape containment. "What?! How?! At this hour?!"

Galen hastily killed the lights and flipped the lock. He skated across the office floor as he dropped to one knee. He softly latched the lab door behind him and retreated down the first bay with the broom closet. The fumbling of loose keys just outside the door brought even more angst to his already tense disposition. Galen prayed it was housekeeping circulating on the floor to empty the trash receptacles. He felt as trapped as a dim-witted thief stealing rubies from a queen's coronation crown during the ceremony.

CHAPTER 19

Three hours, twenty minutes until crating.

At 4:02 A.M., Simon Floundary awoke restlessly. Unable to sleep, he brewed a pot of coffee and conceded to start his workday earlier than expected. Before heading out the door, he threw on a brown lightweight jacket with a small German flag embroidered in the area of a regimental badge. Though an early riser, arriving at work at 4:40 A.M. was a new personal best. Knowing he needed to leave work early for Jesse's procedure in some ways justified arriving well before dawn.

In front of the speckled glass window of his office door, Simon fiddled with his keys. They slipped through his fingers to the floor as he pulled them from his pocket. The jarring jingle of the landing keys broke the hallway's silence and startled Simon from his sleepy lull.

"Please don't come in. Please don't come in," Galen pleaded as he lightly crept backward away from the lab door toward the closet.

The echo of the keys had vanished. The hallway fell silent again. As Simon crouched to reclaim the keys, he heard a clatter from behind his office door. Galen's olecranon[35] had struck a rack of test tubes on the workbench. The glass tubes rang out like a percussionist playing carillon chimes.

Simon turned the key in the lock. Fearing a mouse may scurry between his feet, he positioned himself at arm's length from the doorknob before cracking it open. He studied the floor waiting for a critter to scurry past, but nothing happened. Simon shoved open the door with so much force that it sprang back partway from the baseboard's doorstop. Still feeling skittish, Simon flicked on the lights and meticulously scanned the room.

As a rim of light poured into the lab from beneath the solid wooden door, Galen scoured the laboratory for any sort of makeshift diversion. The last thing he wanted was to confront a living stranger face-to-face. He needed to escape unnoticed, but how? He had literally backed himself into a corner with no place to flee except for a broom closet. Hiding for too long would inevitably put Tome and Marcel at risk. Convincing this interloper he was from housekeeping wasn't exactly an option.

At a neighboring workstation in the next bay over, a contained liquid emitted a faint lime green glow. The dim light was just enough to read the beaker's label, *Green Fluorescent Protein*. Thinking quickly, Galen grabbed the bioluminescent suspension and a pipette.

---

[35] The olecranon is the ulna's bony eminence that forms the pointed portion of the elbow. The olecranon is the lever the triceps brachii muscle uses to extend the forearm.

Starting at the lab door, he released penny-sized droplets of the suspension on the floor like a trail of breadcrumbs leading to nowhere. He strategically routed the trail of glowing globules to the far back corner of the lab, the furthest distance away from the broom closet. For added effect, Galen plotted the outline of an arrowhead that pointed to a nondescript alcove. The recessed area was a workspace outfitted with a rolling chair, a low black countertop to match the lab's otherwise waist-high countertops, and a corkboard wall with a photo and experiment schedule tacked to it.

Hearing the commotion in the office, Galen fled to the closet. One more barrier was now between him and whoever was on the other side. Distressed and hopeless, Galen rested his forehead and hands against the inner closet door. He took a deep airless breath and contemplated his next move hoping his impromptu ingenuity would be enough to avoid an unpleasant and possibly threatening confrontation. "Could this be it?" Galen considered, knowing this may be his final demise. As he extended his cervical spine to raise his head, the lab door creaked open sending a haunting chill through Galen's bone marrow.

Before Simon stepped foot into the lab, his eyes were drawn to the glowing droplets like a moth drawn to light. Simon's suspicious gaze scanned the room, but the lure of the fluorescent trail was too much for him to resist.

With the closet door partially cracked, Galen pressed his ear to the opening to count the clacks of Simon's dress shoes. Galen knew the exact number of droplets he had placed at intervals the same distance as his own stride length. Four more steps. Galen waited in anticipation as he crouched ready for an abrupt exit.

Simon stopped at the tip of the arrowhead bewildered by the trail's unremarkable ending which led him to his former graduate student's desk. Perplexed and uncertain of what to do, Simon carefully studied the bulletin board in front of him. A strip of paper held in place by two thumbtacks displayed a short passage of text that read, "Do not withhold good from those who deserve it when it is in your power to help them. Proverbs 3:27." Simon's moment of contemplation was abruptly disrupted when the lab door drew his attention. The door casually opened wider than he had left it, as if by its own free will.

Simon returned to his office and browsed the room for a second time. Everything appeared in its place, just as he had left it.

Galen, just out of view in the hallway under the edge of the speckled glass window, caught the scent of Simon's cologne as he swept past his jacket on the coat rack. He detected notes of bergamot and suede. Simon's cell phone rang startling Galen. He tried to regain his composure but found it difficult to gauge his stress level without feeling the beat of his own heart. Despite knowing better, Galen lingered to eavesdrop.

Elena's photo lit up on Simon's display. He figured she was calling out of concern having woken up alone in bed. With a heavy sigh, Simon answered on speaker-phone, "Hi, love… No, I'm fine. I just couldn't sleep. I'm getting a head start at the office so I can leave early for Jesse's procedure." Though she sounded like a muffled chipmunk, Galen detected concern in the woman's voice. Much to Galen's surprise, Simon ended the call faster than a competitive eating champion devouring a hotdog.

Realizing the unproductiveness of his snooping, Galen sprang up and darted to the stairwell with Vitalis-like speed. He furtively depressed the stairwell door's panic bar with his thenar eminence[36] and climbed the stairs two steps at a time.

Simon walked around the side of his desk where he had rested his brown leather satchel. He paused with alarm when he found his computer screen lit, showing his drug trial database. The entry line read <ORGAN.

"Organ? Really?" Simon bemoaned as he recalled the heart-wrenching organ donation conversation with Dr. Cramer. To be reminded of a thought he had worked so hard to suppress infuriated him. Simon rolled his desk chair up close to the keyboard. He immediately closed the database to purge the irritating thought from his mind.

To suppress his emotions, Simon opened a research manuscript on his desktop and began writing a discussion section until he noticed a rogue pamphlet lying to the left of his keyboard. Simon picked up the flyer, curious about its origin. The cardstock showed a white gift

---

[36] The thenar eminence is a mound of three muscles at the base of the thumb on the palm of the hand.

package wrapped with a crimson red bow. The brochure read, *'Let the good in you live on'* and outlined five reasons to pass along the gift of life through organ donation. Despite feeling a surge of disgruntlement, Simon loathingly and skeptically read the entire pamphlet, mostly hoping to fact-check Dr. Cramer's earlier claims. Reluctant to admit it, Dr. Cramer's information was valid.

Simon flipped over the leaflet. The reverse side was blank, except for his computer password scribbled at the top of the page. Simon leaned back in his office chair, mystified by the entire circumstance.

Galen burst into the cadaver lab to find Tome pulling out one of his cross-sections to demonstrate his organs from the viewpoint of a CT scanner. Maurice had never seen the body from this perspective before. Marcel, leaning nonchalantly on a cadaver tank, chatted up Gloria.

"We have to leave now!" Galen vociferated in a winded voice. "Simon is in the building. I was almost caught red-handed." Shocked by the unexpected news, Marcel and Tome stood frozen in disbelief, just as still as their moritati poses.

"I have the Ribozore, but the drug trial did not have Morgan listed as a participant. As I typed her name into the registry, I heard a commotion in the hallway. Then, someone, whom I think was Dr. Simon Floundary, entered the office. I had no choice but to retreat." The words spewed from Galen's mouth faster than a raging waterfall. "Where are the scrubs?" Marcel pointed to a nondescript lateral file cabinet at the edge of the room. "Let's get changed and head out."

The three discarded Vitalis's museum finds to don mint green scrubs for a more casual but professional look. Galen strategically clipped Arden's badge to his shirt pocket for added effect. As they changed their attire, they devised a plan to reenter the tunnel plexus, the most logical and efficient of the options.

Before leaving the cadaver lab, the trio thanked Gloria and Maurice for their hospitality. Looking back at Gloria, Marcel contracted his orbicularis oculi muscle[37] as he gestured a wink. Then, with his orbicularis oris muscle,[38] he pursed his lips to deliver a kind-hearted kiss through the thick fixative-ladened air. Both hoped they would one day meet again.

"We're leaving the lab and are en route to the hospital," Galen called over the two-way radio to check in with Cato.

The team returned to the tunnel system to capitalize on the direct connection between the buildings. As they raced through the concrete plexus, Galen's morale wavered. He held tight to the vial of Ribozore, all the while knowing he had failed to enter Morgan's name as a treatment group participant. The only hope he had left was to give Morgan a full dose of Ribozore to kick-start her heart's cellular restructuring. At that moment, the vial represented life itself. It symbolized the hope of a future for his late crush, who meant the world to him. If

---

[37] The orbicularis oculi muscles encircle each orbit and close the eyelids.
[38] The orbicularis oris muscle encircles the mouth and functions to purse the lips.

the vessels of Cameo's skin had been anastomosed to Galen's, a visible blush would have appeared at the thought of calling Morgan his crush. He shook off the thought like a dog shaking its wet fur coat. He knew the fight to save her was not over yet. His determination kept him keenly focused on the task until his feelings for Morgan recaptured him like an unwieldy vine. How could he see her again and not want to tell her everything, including how he felt about her? What if she was awake? Might he have to stick her with a needle to administer the Ribozore? What once felt like an infallible plan was suddenly unraveling like a de-leathered baseball.

The retracting doors marking the transition into the hospital's subbasement were embossed with the caduceus symbol. They automatically recoiled as Galen approached revealing a spacious, well-lit passageway. Extra hospital beds and IV poles lined the walls as if the hospital had run out of storage space. A series of electronic medication carts plugged into waist-high wall outlets looked like boats moored to a dock. At the end of the corridor, the team stopped just outside of the entryway to the hospital's morgue.

Galen repeatedly stabbed the backlit button as if to hasten the elevator's descent. The car ignored the palpable urgency as it costively lowered one floor at a time to the sub-basement.

Marcel's frontalis muscles[39] raised his eyebrows as he

---

[39] The frontalis muscle raises the eyebrows and wrinkles the forehead. As the saying goes, "Nothing raises eyebrows like frontalis."

exchanged a glance of elation with Tome. With a smug grin, he pointed to the morgue excited at the prospect of meeting other fellow specimens. "What a place to kill time," Marcel joked, unable to resist the pun as the three waited for the agonizingly sluggish lift.

"Not now, you two," Galen blurted. "We have to get upstairs." Having visited Morgan at the hospital on prior occasions, Galen finally felt a sense of normalcy, at least as much as one could, given the circumstances. He knew his whereabouts, more or less, and felt confident in his ability to swiftly navigate the team to the cardiac unit.

At the elevator's tuneful chime, the three raced in, feeling another déjà vu moment. As the lift ascended, Galen closed his eyes, realizing the distance to reaching Morgan decreased with every passing second. Marcel patted Galen on the back stimulating Galen's mechano-receptors, calming his psyche. Tome and Marcel felt they were living vicariously through Galen's roller-coaster ride of emotions, something they vaguely re-called only experiencing in life.

As Galen opened his eyes, a nagging memory flashed to the forefront of his mind. The last time he rode this elevator, he held a bouquet of tie-dyed roses for Morgan. He had finally mustered enough courage to ask her to the winter formal. However, once he had finally found her room, three incessant nurses were hovering over her assessing her condition. He couldn't bear the added pressure of three middle-aged women aahing over his sweet attempt to woo a young and attractive patient to a frivolous high school dance. He left the flowers in the record holder outside the door and disappeared undetected. Galen convinced himself, this time, the outcome would be different. It had to be different for Morgan's sake. With the cure in hand and wherewithal to intervene, this time he could not allow his secret timidness to interfere.

CHAPTER 20

BONE ASH

One hour forty-five minutes until crating.

The trio stepped out of the elevator and entered the butterfly-shaped cardiac unit. Four corridors of rooms emerged from a centralized node that housed the nurses' monitoring stations. Waiting lounges and private consultation spaces occupied the four points of the butterfly's wings. Galen looked frantic. He had not recalled there being so many rooms from his memories of visiting Morgan. The volume of possibilities outnumbered the time they had remaining. Visiting each room one by one to locate Morgan was out of the question. "Bring it in," Galen called. The three huddled together to strategize.

"If we split up and search each room, it may look suspicious," Tome interjected first.

"Can we access a nurse's station to look her up in the system?" suggested Galen.

"There are nurses and staff everywhere. Simply wearing scrubs may not be enough to blend in while pecking away on someone's keyboard," Tome rebutted.

Marcel listened intently, synthesizing all the possibilities.

"There is no perfect solution," Galen admitted in a deflated tone. "We're so close, but we still need one last Hail Mary." He wiped his hands across his scrub bottoms as if he had sweaty palms, despite Cameo's skin being denervated.

Marcel traipsed back and forth to the side of the huddle with his hands clenched behind his back. He knew there was only one option. "Come with me," he said assuredly to Galen and Tome. They both followed suit, not realizing his intentions.

The trio approached a nurse standing at a nearby workstation. A fresh bouquet of scarlet roses in a clear crystal vase enriched the otherwise bare ledge of her bureau. Galen tried to ignore the roses as they only reminded him of his cowardliness. Marcel drew near to the nurse with unwavering confidence. Upon realizing Marcel's intent, Tome lunged for his shoulder to stop him, but it was too late.

Marcel shook like a patient with Parkinson's disease. He stiffened to quell the trimmer. "Hello, miss," Marcel spoke directly to the nurse. His vocal folds tightened and quivered in his larynx as fear emerged between them. His tremble escalated to an audible and awkward stammer. "I'm part of D-Dr. Floundary's research team. He asked me to ch-check on one of our patients who is a potential candidate for o-our study, Morgan Lowe. I-I've never been to this u-unit before. Could you point me to her rrroom?"

Marcel visibly tensed his body to concentrate on holding himself together. The nurse scrolled through the patients' inventory on her computer. "Ah, here she is. Morgan is in room 718," she replied, just loud enough for Galen and Tome to overhear.

"Th- Thhhank you," Marcel stuttered as he turned away from the kiosk. Galen and Tome stood awestruck. Their hearts sank into their chests as they grappled with the impending consequence of Marcel's actions.

As Marcel ambulated toward them, the individual tissues and cells comprising his body separated like dust particles visible in a ray of sunlight. His entire body and mint green scrubs transfigured into ash as naturally as an extinguished flame fading to smoke. Marcel's remains slowly wafted to the floor. In the twinkling of an eye, the small mound of bone ash dissipated and nearly vanished, leaving behind only a residue of soot. The Code of Silence took him at its will.

Galen winced at the thought of his selfish escapade causing a fatality. Tome grabbed Galen's shoulder and they both bowed their heads aghast, regretting they had not intervened sooner. Galen stood motionless and distraught. Marcel's departure called to mind the reality of death and the preciousness of life.

"He knew what he was doing. Marcel believed in you and the mission," Tome consoled Galen.

In reflective solitude, Galen withdrew a single rose from the vase atop the nurse's workstation. He felt an obligatory need to memorialize Marcel's altruistic sacrifice. With grace and humility, Galen knelt and placed rose petals on the soot in the exact location where Marcel dematerialized. The memorial was befitting and symbolized the completion of Marcel's human finality. The rose petals gradually dissolved into the soot as if Marcel had accepted Galen's peace offering.

Down the hall from the nurse's workstation, the entrance to Morgan's hospital room was viewable from the visitors' waiting area. Tome recognized the magnitude of the moment for Galen. He kept a watchful eye on Galen and the room from the visitors' lounge where he cleverly hid behind a magazine. On the magazine's cover was a close-up of the country's most notorious wrestler. An encrypted barcode tattoo ran obliquely across his face from his forehead to the body of his mandible. His sharply shaven goatee looked like the pinchers of a fierce arthropod. Tome held the magazine at the perfect angle. The wrestler's head appeared conjoined to Tome's body, creating a humorous optical illusion from a distance.

Before Galen entered the room, he paused, looked back at Tome, and took a deep breath as if to calm his nerves. Tome observed a mild tremor in Galen's hand holding the medication vial. As silent as an owl stalking its prey, Galen entered the room and gingerly latched the door behind him. Overcome with emotion, he firmly clenched his teeth as his chin quivered at the sight of Morgan. Morgan's grandmother, Amelia Lowe, lay reclined in the hideous mustard-yellow chair in the far corner of the room. Her hearing aids and clip-on earrings rested on the windowsill. Morgan slept curled into a ball with her arms pulled in tight. Her disheveled covers implied she had had a restless night. Galen stood in the shadows admiring Morgan for her inner beauty.

As a cloud eclipsed the moon's glow, Galen suddenly felt dizzy and disoriented. The onset of the conversion clutched him like a ravaged phantom strangling him of his consciousness. He felt his memories being eradicated one at a time, like an insecticide wafting into the deepest reaches of an ants' nest. As if he were wading upstream against a torrent of personal memories and emotions, Galen physically braced himself. He pressed his hand firmly against his temple to quell the pain. Attempting to dissuade the conversion and determined to complete the mission, he dragged himself to Morgan's bedside, his head throbbing.

Galen pulled the needle and antique glass syringe from his bag. His equilibrium wavered. He consciously contracted his quadriceps to prevent his knees from buckling. Galen held the vial at eye level to withdraw the Ribozore. Before the needle's beveled tip could pierce the vial's stopper, Morgan suddenly muttered in her sleep, "Got ya last!" Already on edge, the sweet yet unexpected sound of Morgan's voice startled Galen. His core shook so violently that the ampule of medication slipped from his grasp. His mind flooded with warm, fond memories of Morgan, especially her bright beaming smile. As if time had slowed to a crawl, Galen watched stunned as gravity took hold of the medication vial and thrust it forcibly to the ground. The glass shattered so diffusely it looked like rock salt cast at Galen's feet. The sound of the pulverizing glass pulled Morgan from her worry-free dream to the reality of her condition. Amelia, as deaf as a post without her hearing aids, slept undisturbed.

Morgan rubbed and squinted her eyes. Galen smiled from ear to ear as Morgan stirred in her bed. Cameo's slack skin made his smile look more like a goofy smirk. Morgan glanced up and cowered as she stared into the lifeless face of a stranger. Fear coiled around her like a giant python. Before she could utter a shrill, Galen covered her mouth with a cupped hand. Morgan instinctively gripped his wrist to peel his hands from her face, but Galen overpowered her. He forced Morgan's lips into a pucker and landed a sloppy uncoordinated smooch like a blindfolded boy bobbing for apples, missing half of her lips.

Galen secretly hoped Morgan would fall limp, overwhelmed by his bold romantic outburst. Instead, Morgan's free hand met Galen's cold loose lips with a forceful slap. Cameo's baggy skin skidded out of alignment with Galen's face. Cameo's nose projected laterally from Galen's cheekbone.

After awkwardly readjusting his face, Galen leaned in again, this time taking a more subtle approach. His right hand costively reached in the direction of Morgan's face. He causally tucked Morgan's long bangs behind her ear. Morgan instantaneously gasped. Only one person in her entire life was particular about the placement of her bangs. She timidly placed her hands around Galen's and fixed her eyes on her guest's pupils, hoping that in some way it would reveal the soul from within.

"Gavin?" Morgan cried in a vibrato whisper, uncertain of her instinct.

Galen removed the mask of Cameo's face like doffing a hood to unveil his more familiar contours. He nodded to Morgan in confirmation. Though his appearance was indistinctly foreign, a pang in Morgan's heart affirmed the implausible. She sniffled and blinked back tears of joy.

"How can this be? I was there. I saw the car careen into you. There was a funeral and everything," Morgan's thoughts gushed out loud like an erupting geyser. "Am I hallucinating?" Feeling lightheaded, she leaned back in the bed. Then, without warning, her face twisted into a tight knot. "Is this some sick prank? Who do you think you are trifling with my emotions?" Morgan barked, hardly able to look Galen in the face. "At the café that day, I wanted to make *us* official. I'm such a fool to fall for a jerk like you who would go to such outlandish extremes to laugh at my expense." The thought of being intentionally deceived utterly repulsed Morgan.

Galen's body and mind froze at the thought of having been so close at the café to finally express their affection for one another. He never truly knew whether the feelings he had for Morgan were reciprocated. Now, the disgusted look on Morgan's face said it all. It would take far more than a box of her favorite Girl Scout cookies to expunge the disappointment in her eyes.

With open palms, Galen gestured *stop* in front of Morgan. His heart screamed internally, "It's not what you think," yet his vocal folds remained inert out of fear of breaking the Code of Silence. The last thing he wanted was to vanish indefinitely into a pile of ash in front of her. Galen's body shuddered uncontrollably. The transformation's unrelenting grip pulled on Galen's memories again like a demon consuming one's being.

"What are you doing? Why are you shaking?" Morgan sat up alarmed at Galen's behavior. "You're scaring me. Say something!" Morgan insisted, her attitude growing incredibly impatient. Galen regained control of his fasciculations. "If you really are Gavin, why would you think you could just come here, kiss me, and not have the decency to explain any of this?"

Galen, nervous that Morgan's snappy rant would wake her grandmother, frantically scrambled for another way to stonewall Morgan's frustrations and to further convince her it was him. A prescription slip lying on the bedside table gave him the perfect idea. Morgan watched Galen's profile as he fiddled with a flimsy piece of paper on the nightstand. After a few short moments, Galen turned back to Morgan who fashioned a stare of disbelief. He cradled an origami swan. As he tugged on the pointed tail, the bird's wings flapped like a youngling warily taking its first flight. To Morgan, the stranger's identity and surreal humor were undeniable.

Galen doubled over clenching his chest and dropped the origami keepsake on her lap. Though he longed to remain at Morgan's side for eternity, the overwhelming pain of his transformation was more than he could physically bear. With foggy vision, he rested his heavy hands on Morgan's shoulders and carefully studied her face, making note of the shape of her nose, the arches of her eyebrows, and the beauty of her endearing smile. Aside from her disheveled auburn hair, she was exactly as he had remembered her. Mentally, Galen incessantly fought back the uprooting of his fading memories craning his neck from side to side hoping to forever seal this moment in time. Sensing Galen's extreme discomfort, Morgan empathetically massaged Galen's temples with her thumbs hoping to dull his pain. Galen closed his eyes and savored the fleeting moment. Despite Morgan's sheer bewilderment, to her, the cozy moment felt right. It felt warm and serene. Without warning, Galen receded from Morgan's bedside and careened to the door like a fishing skiff drifting from the comforts of port into the throes of the Bering Sea.

"Wait!" Morgan shouted in a strained whisper. She reached for the side table.

Galen turned one last time to treasure his first love's expression. As he did, Morgan's bracelet flew as straight as an arrow at his head. He caught it reflexively in mid-air as it whirled past the pinna of his ear. "I'll always be your diamond in the rough," Morgan promised, reminding Galen how much he meant to her.

In return, wishing he could undo his reckless kiss, Galen flashed an "I love you" in sign language. It felt as if time itself had stopped.

Morgan watched in a lonely and perplexed silence as Galen vanished through the doorway. Lavished by a flood of emotions, never had she felt such intense joy coupled with such deep heartache and despair. The encounter, while immensely gratifying, left her utterly puzzled and yearning to understand how the impossible felt so real.

Galen staggered out of room 718. His head felt like it was trapped in an unrelenting vice. Barely able to fix his gaze on any one object, he scanned the unit for Tome. Like a trainer ushering an injured athlete from the playing field, Tome swooped in from behind and flung Galen's arm over his shoulders.

"I've got you," assured Tome as he escorted Galen to the shelter of the nearest stairwell. Just as Tome pressed Galen's back against the concrete wall to seat him, Galen fainted.

CHAPTER 21

OPUS VITAE

Simon Floundary rubbed his forehead. His poor night's sleep made his eyes particularly sensitive to the fluorescent lights lining the cardiac unit's hallway.

"Good morning Dr. Floundary," said a nurse walking out of a patient's room. She dispensed sanitizer into the palm of her hand at the nursing station. "This is certainly a surprise! You never stop by to visit us this early."

"It's nice to see you, too," Dr. Floundary replied. "I need to tie up a few loose ends before I take a few days of vacation to spend with Jesse. His surgery is this afternoon."

"I hope everything goes smoothly. I'm sure Jesse will be in good hands with our neuro team." The nurse stepped away from the unit's check-in desk. She turned back to Dr. Floundary. "Oh. I forgot to mention, I met one of your research assistants this morning. He had a terrible stutter and seemed a little fretful for some reason."

"Really?" returned Simon as his head swiveled with intrigue. "I don't currently have a research assistant.

What did this individual have to say?"

"He was looking for one of your patients."

"That's peculiar. Do you know which patient?" Simon questioned with growing concern.

"Sure, I remember the room number perfectly. It happens to be my birthday. Room 718."

"Thanks. If you don't mind, I'll check in on the patient." He was already in motion heading in the room's direction.

Dr. Floundary barged into room 718 without even knocking. His abruptness startled Amelia Lowe so much that she catapulted herself into an upright position from the mustard-yellow recliner.

"I'm sorry to have alarmed you," Dr. Floundary apologized, realizing his gruff entrance. "If I may ask, has anyone visited your room this morning other than the typical nursing staff?"

"I'm sorry, sir, but who are you?" Amelia Lowe asked as she frantically seated her hearing aids in her external auditory meatuses.

"No, Dr. Floundary!" Morgan's said impulsively. "You're the first person to wake us up this morning. Don't you know it's before 7 A.M.? You never wake a teenage girl before 7 A.M. It's an unwritten rule."

As Dr. Floundary turned to address Amelia, Morgan pondered her imaginative dream. For good measure, she glanced over the bedside with sloth-like speed to peek at the floor. Morgan respired deeply at the sight of glass shards and a puddle of clear liquid the size of a melted ice cube.

Amelia Lowe turned her attention to Morgan. "Are you alright, dear?"

Morgan gave a snippy reply, "I'm fine!" She sat up in her hospital bed and pulled the covers close to her chest. Amelia furrowed her brow at Morgan as she turned back to the conversation with Dr. Floundary.

Morgan looked at the bedside table. A crudely constructed origami swan sat in the place where she had laid aside her charm bracelet the night before. While Dr. Floundary's attention was still on her grandmother, Morgan sat up and dangled her legs off the edge of the bed until her tiptoes touched the tiled floor. She inconspicuously swept the glass fragments and residual liquid under the bed with her bare feet away from Simon's view.

Morgan overheard Simon, "The main reason I'm here this morning is to follow up on your family's interest to enroll Morgan in a new drug trial."

"I'll do it!" stated Morgan emphatically.

"I'm glad you're enthusiastic about the trial, but I must receive consent from your legal guardians."

"What's the name of the medication, anyway?" asked Morgan.

"It's called Ribozore," said Dr. Floundary in a very proud manner.

"I'm sorry, Dr. Floundary, but Morgan's mother isn't here right now, and only she can provide the consent you're seeking," Amelia explained.

Simon Floundary had been in this position before. He knew all too well that educating extended family members often benefited his study recruitment efforts. Simon took the opportunity to share the research trial's specifics with Amelia and made a compelling argument for why Morgan was an ideal candidate. Almost verbatim, he repeated the same information he had previously shared with Morgan's mother, Mina.

While Simon rambled on about the study and the recruitment process, Morgan nonchalantly slid from the edge of the bed onto the floor. She tugged on her EKG lines to stretch them as far as they could reach. On her knees, she peered under the bed, hoping to find visible markings on a piece of the shattered glass. Much to her surprise, she found something even better – a medication label. It read, *Ribozore*. It was all starting to make sense, at least the part where Gavin wanted her to have the medication. Still, his visible appearance and his existence after the fatal accident were a baffling conundrum.

As Morgan arose from the floor, she spotted a leaflet of paper tucked away in Dr. Floundary's lab coat pocket. It showed an image of a white gift package wrapped with a crimson red bow. As if she had no manners, Morgan pried into Simon's personal bubble. "What's that in your pocket?" She pointed directly at the flyer. "Christmas is still several months away."

Taken aback by Morgan's question, Simon faltered with a response, "Uhh...it has nothing to do with Christmas."

Simon tried to restart his spiel about the study with Amelia, but Morgan's curiosity got the best of her. "But it has a present wrapped with a bow on it. If it's not about Christmas, then what's it for?"

Simon paused, internally debating if he should brush her off again or answer her question. With great reluctance and a huff, Simon answered, "It's a flyer about organ donations."

"We donated my father's body to science," Morgan stated as a matter of fact.

Amelia inserted herself. "My son, Morgan's father, passed away three years ago from a tragic accident at the factory he oversaw. In his final hours, the doctors told us he had a relentless grit to survive. Unfortunately, the internal injuries he sustained were more than his body could handle." Feeling nervously uncomfortable with the conversation, Simon fidgeted with the chattering keys in his pocket. "He always brought out the best in people and always put others before himself." Amelia softly cleared her throat to hide her quavering voice. "He cherished life and his children. No matter the difficulties he encountered. My son always pressed through with a positive attitude and an unwavering will to succeed." Dr. Floundary nodded, mostly as a sign of respect for Amelia's grief. "My daughter-in-law, Mina, felt that donating his body was the right thing to do. She consented for his body to be used for medical education and research. For her, it represented a final act of true love. Mina wanted her husband's zest for life to symbolically live on in a different, but equally powerful way."

Mindful of proper patient etiquette, Simon obligatorily stepped to Morgan's bedside. His hands crossed in front of him at his waist. "Your father sounds like an extraordinary man. He reminds me of my son in many ways." As Simon shifted his weight, he heard a sound like the crunching of peanut brittle beneath the sole of his wing-tipped dress shoe. He raised his foot as if he had stepped in a wad of bubble gum. Simon glanced at the broken ampule barely visible from beneath the bed.

"What's this?" Dr. Floundary crouched down for a closer visual. He glared at the label attached to the largest shard of glass. "How did you acquire this?" His tone was no longer cordial.

"I don't know what you're talking about. I've never seen it before," responded Morgan, who looked to her grandmother for support.

Simon became infuriated. His blood pressure spiked to an unhealthy level. "These vials represent my entire opus vitae [life's work]. If patients who are not enrolled in the trial receive this medication, I could be investigated by the Federal Institute for Drugs and Medical Devices. I could lose everything – my drug license, my research, my tenure. The whole drug trial could be jeopardized, setting us back months if not years."

Amelia looked sternly at the irate researcher. "Dr. Floundary, as Morgan has already explained, no one has been in our room. We were sound asleep until you charged in rudely awakening us. I'm sorry, but I think we've heard enough about the drug trial. I think it's best if you leave now."

"But I want to be in the trial. I need the medication," Morgan pleaded, her face tense with determination. "I can't explain it, but I know I need to be a part of the trial!"

"Morgan, that's a discussion to have with your mother. Good day, Dr. Floundary," Amelia asserted as she physically positioned herself in between them. Amelia stared holes through Dr. Floundary's back as he bolted for the door.

CHAPTER 22

ENTANGLED

One hour until crating.

In the stairwell, Tome gently slapped Galen's cheeks to rouse him. Galen remained slumped over so groggy he could hardly open his eyes, yet he heard Tome calling his name. He finally regained full alertness.

"Galen, are you okay? How are you feeling?" Tome asked, concerned the mission may have rendered another casualty.

"I think it's over. I think the transformation is complete," eeked Galen, stunned by the fury of the final conversion. I have a dull headache, but it's nothing like what I just experienced."

"What's this?" asked Tome as he nudged at the bracelet dangling from the handle strap of Galen's leather bag.

"It's Morgan's bracelet. She wanted me to have it to remember her by," Galen said with a glowing smile.

"Wait. What happened in there? And how do you still know Morgan's name? You didn't speak to her, did you?" Tome had more questions than his mouth could keep up with.

"I'll explain once we get back. No, I did not verbally speak to her. If I had, would I be talking to you right now?" Galen remarked. "As for how or why I remember her name, I'm not certain. But I'm glad I do."

Contemplating the phenomenon, Tome theorized, "Well, when the final transformation occurs, we remember all aspects of our new life from that point forward. Because you interacted with Morgan during your transformation, it's plausible that your past memories have now become entangled with your new persona. No other body has been in contact with their past life at the time of their transformation. You're an n of one. It's the only possible explanation."

Over the hospital intercom, an automated female voice announced, "Your attention, please. Code gray. Cardiac unit. Seventh floor."

Galen hastily accepted Tome's theory until another explanation could present itself. "We can't waste any more time. We need to get back to the museum," Galen urged. "We have to go now!"

The overhead voice rang out once more, "Code gray. Cardiac unit. Seventh floor."

The duo descended the stairs toward the hospital's ground-floor lobby only as fast as Galen's overtaxed body would allow. At the third level, they were met by the footsteps of heavy work boots rapidly ascending the stairs. Galen and Tome pulled themselves to the same side of the stairwell allowing the enthusiastic stair climber to pass. When Tome got a closer look at the passerby, he uncontrollably gasped in panic. Trying to cover up Tome's surprised expression, Galen gave a large cordial smile and a polite hand wave.

The passerby, a clean-shaven security officer with bright yellow sporty sunglasses, halted on the landing. "Good morning gentlemen," he replied in a calm and collected voice acknowledging Galen's wave.

The duo casually continued their descent acting un-ruffled by the encounter. The security officer advanced in the opposite direction. Once out of sight, they hurried their pace until they reached the subbasement.

"That was too close for comfort," Tome couldn't re-sist expressing the obvious.

"If I had a working urinary system, I'm pretty sure I would have peed my pants back there," Galen admitted.

CHAPTER 23

STAR-CROSSED LOVERS

The entire bus ride, Galen sat silent and depressed as he continuously replayed every one of the mission's failures in his mind. Tome whispered over the walkie-talkie, "We're on Old Bridge. We're two bus stops away from the museum. Wake the guards."

Excited to receive another communication from the team, Cato responded immediately to the call. "Roger that." He turned to the others. "It's time to free the guards." Cameo and Cassius hustled to the plastination room.

"After we close the gas valve, how long will it take for them to recover?" asked Cameo.

"It's hard to say," replied Cassius. "We've never done this before. If they wake too quickly, the others may not get back to their platforms in time. If they recover too slowly, the guards on the morning shift might find them incapacitated."

"Well, here goes nothing." Cameo shut off the valve to the curing gas canister. "It's a good thing we didn't capture them any earlier. There's hardly any gas left." The pressure gauge hovered dangerously close to zero.

"Help me untie them," urged Cassius.

"Wait!" exclaimed Cameo. "Let's roll them to the breakroom and set them on the couch. They'll think they fell asleep on break."

"Not a bad idea."

Cassius and Cameo expediently shuttled the dazed guards, perched on rolling office chairs, to the break room. "Having dead bodies transport living bodies, now that's irony," remarked Cameo. "Just saying."

The two plastinates strategically placed the guards in a restful position on an antiquated maroon leather couch. Unable to help himself, Cameo carefully entangled the guards' fingers together one digit at a time. When he finished positioning them, they looked like star-crossed lovers cuddled up for a featured film. Cameo even got a modest grin to stick on the younger guard's face.

After slipping the iPhone in the younger guard's top pocket, Cameo and Cassius made their exit. The guards stirred when the door slammed against its frame. They sluggishly awoke, dazed, and confused. Their bodies felt heavy as if they had the strength of a small child trying to lift a grown man's arm. Once all sensations of tactile feeling and proprioception returned, they soon realized their bodies' dispositions. Cameo had nestled them so close to one another the younger guard could smell the veteran's raunchy breath. It reeked of garlic. In unison, each retreated to the farthest reaches of the couch. As the senior guardsman slid across the couch cushions, he intended to extend his wrist as he reached for the armrest. Instead, the dorsum of his hand slapped hard against the couch's leather arm, pushing his wrist into hyperflexion. After rubbing away the carpal pain, he held both hands out in front of him. His left hand was as limp as a dead flower. The range of motion in his right hand and wrist were normal. Unbeknown to the guard, he suffered a radial nerve palsy from Cameo's positioning of his axilla over the chair.

"What time is it?" questioned the rookie. "Do you remember anything that happened last night?"

"I vaguely remember there being an alarm of some kind," recalled the senior guard, still perplexed, and bothered by the unresponsiveness of his left hand.

"I don't hear it now. We must have tended to it and then took a break," rationalized the rookie. "But I've never fallen asleep on the job before."

"There's a first for everything," replied the elder guard, peering at the large digital time display sitting on a metal locker in the corner of the breakroom. "It's 6:57. The next shift and the shipping company will be here soon. We need to complete our rounds to ensure everything is safe and sound. You take the upper four floors. I'll take the lower."

Both guards proceeded to the task. Already embarrassed by having laid dormant most of the evening, the rookie chose not to recount his unease with the eighth floor. Dutifully, he headed straight to the top floor to prevent prolonging his discomfort. From the periphery of the Plastination Planet exhibit, all the displayed specimens looked peaceful and resolute in their assigned poses. The rookie performed a quick sweep. He snaked through only half of the exhibit knowing he was pressed for time. He cruised five feet past Cassius when he stopped dead in his tracks and reversed course. He stood directly in front of Cassius and carefully inspected him from head to toe.

"You look familiar," the rookie murmured aloud. Despite his critical scrutiny of the specimen, he could not discern why he felt more connected to this particular body than any other. Checking his watch, he moved on, missing the three empty platforms kitty-corner from Cassius's display.

CHAPTER 24

LIFE'S JOURNEY

Thirty minutes until crating.

Galen pressed his pterion[40] against the bus window. His eyes rapidly jerked as they fixated on the painted dashed lines demarcating their road lane from the oncoming traffic. Every detail of their visit to the cardiac unit preoccupied his mind. He dissected every step and pondered what he could have done differently to have gotten Morgan the Ribozore she so desperately needed.

"Next stop, museum campus," called the bus driver, this one more cheerful than the first.

With a flexed and ridged forearm, Tome extended his hand to offer Galen extra leverage from his seat. Galen stood like a flimsy puppet. His body language mimicked that of a listless zombie. Failure filled Galen with such despair even his feet felt weighed down by a force equivalent to Jupiter's gravity. The modern, fully equipped bus came to a halt. As if engaging the release valve of a car jack, the bus's hydraulics lowered it to the

---

[40] The pterion (ter-ee-on) is the temple of the head and is the weakest area of the lateral skull where four skull bones unite. Forceful trauma to the pterion could cause a rupture of the middle meningeal artery (which courses deep to the pterion) resulting in an epidural hematoma.

ground miniaturizing the descent from the bus's platform to the concrete.

They gazed at the playground they had previously traversed with Marcel only a few short hours ago. Both stood mute as they thought about their friend and his selfless act of courage. Neither was prepared to disclose the news to the other bodies, especially to Arden.

As if they were looking from behind jail bars, Galen and Tome gripped the iron fence lining the perimeter of the play yard. "Well, we can't get back into the museum the way we came out. That exit is locked," Tome admitted, looking past the playground's dig site. The carbon gray door had no visible handle or entry mechanism.

Faintly in the distance, they heard the low rumbling of an idling diesel truck coupled with an occasional disgruntled holler. Curious of the commotion's source, Galen and Tome stealthily walked towards the clamor. At the rear of the museum, the reverberations of a large hauling truck, with its engine idling, echoed off the brick façade's angled contours. It sat parked at the loading dock where the exhibit items were inventoried as they entered and left the building. A partially scuffed and faded decal on the side of the truck read, *Sterling Moving Services, Est. 1952.*

"Vince, can you take a break from sipping your coffee? Give me a hand over here," huffed a stocky man whose head poked out from the truck's open back. Dressed in a gray jumpsuit, the stocky man's baseball cap fashioned the distinctive diamond-patterned logo of Bayern Munich's football club. His hair tried to escape the cap's strangling hold in every direction. A second man appeared from the loading dock's dark abyss wearing the same drab uniform, minus the baseball cap. The lanky fellow exhibited a slight kyphotic posture and sported a bushy mustache darker than a cast-iron skillet. Taking one last sip, he placed the steaming insulated coffee cup on the ledge of the dock and disappeared with his counterpart into the belly of the idling truck.

Galen and Tome exchanged contemplative glances. The loading dock was their best reentry option. They returned their attention to the movers to carefully study their work patterns in hopes of slipping past them at an opportune time. Soon the mismatched pair emerged from the truck. Walking backward, each maneuvered a two-wheeled dolly cradling a large wooden crate from the truck's bed to the concrete dock. The crates were taller than they were wide. Other similar containers akin in shape, but variable in size, rested on the dock's slab floor.

As the squeaking sound of poorly greased dolly casters faded, Tome seized Galen by the wrist. Both sprinted across the asphalt driveway. They crouched for a respite by the front passenger's side wheel. Their unobstructed view of the dock's platform gave them a better visual of the staging area. Just beyond the collection of crates, the movers carted two of the plywood-lined boxes onto a decrepit service elevator and vanished behind a rusty metal curtain.

"Those must be our crates," Tome said with a hint of excitement as he vigorously shook Galen's shoulder.

The front of every crate displayed the word *FRAGILE* stamped at random angles in large red capital letters. A unique alphanumeric code lined the top face of each crate. Near the containers' handles, at waist level, a bold arrow pointed upward over the word *TOP*, as if the crates' tops and bottoms were not already well defined by their other features. "If we each hide in one of the crates, they'll roll us directly to the exhibit hall. It's perfect!" Tome rationalized.

Recognizing their limited time before the movers returned, Tome and Galen crept toward the rear bumper. They crawled onto the dock. The hauler was mostly empty, with only four crates remaining near the truck's cab. They approached the two closest wooden compartments. Six fasteners lined the edges of each crate. Turning a fastener's moth-shaped handle counter-clockwise released its bent hook from its latch. Despite releasing all the latches, the first crate refused to surrender its faceplate. Galen and Tome pried on the cover from every angle with their bare hands. "It's no use," complained Tome, unable to secure a sturdy grip.

"Can you use one of your slices as a pry bar?" Galen asked, grasping at straws.

"They're too thin. The cross-section will snap in two," replied Tome. "What do you have in your leather bag?"

"Nothing strong enough or large enough to gain the needed leverage."

Galen scanned every nook and cranny of the truck, looking between and behind the remaining crates.

Nothing. "They must use something to open these crates. Where is it?" Galen moaned in frustration.

"Maybe it's in the truck's cab."

Finally, Galen spotted a flathead crowbar perched atop the shortest of the crates sitting on the dock. "There!" Galen blurted, his feet already moving in that direction.

"How are you going to resecure the faceplate, so it doesn't pop off?" Tome asked as they inspected the crate's interior.

"I'll have to grip the cross brace to prevent it from opening." Galen pointed to the piece of horizontal wood fortifying the inside of the crate's cover. "Come on. I'll seal you in."

Tome did as he was instructed. Galen quickly fastened all the latches at the frame's edge. For the second crate, Galen only unlatched the fasteners on one side to use the remaining latches as makeshift hinges. After manipulating his body with contortionist-like moves to squeeze inside, he pulled the cover tight against the frame. The confined quarters reminded him of his white sheet experience in the plastination room.

The movers returned to the truck before Galen had a chance to exhale inside the crate. The lanky man's pursed lips whistled *Sittin' On the Dock of the Bay*. Only he saw the humor in it. "Aren't we done yet?" the stout man said. He shuffled his feet as he slid the plate of the two-wheeled hand cart under Tome's upright casket. "My back is killing me. I need some ibuprofen." The stout man held his lumbar spine wincing in pain as he arched his back, laterally flexed his trunk, and took a bow to stretch his erector spinae muscles.[41]

"Those last four empty crates are for the sculptures at the art museum. Close and latch the door," said the lanky man's gnarly mustache. "We'll head there next as soon as we're done moving these crates upstairs." The box truck's overhead door aggressively rolled down its tracks. A resounding thud and the clack of the latch handle signaled the door's unmistakable closure.

Tome, with his ear pressed firmly against the plywood's interior, went ballistic. "Galen, we're stranded," Tome exclaimed, his voice muffled by the enclosure. Tome beat feverishly against the box, like dueling mallets striking a marching bass drum.

"Calm down," Galen voiced, a bit frantic himself as he squeezed back out of the crate through the narrow fissure. Galen reclaimed the crowbar from the floor, though he didn't need it. Tome's overwrought enthusiasm was no match for the crate's stubborn faceplate. The panel burst away from the wooden enclosure like a portly linebacker plowing over a display mannequin. Tome's slices dispersed in every direction. The truck's bed looked like someone had set off an explosion of Frisbee discs of every imaginable size. "Get yourself together," Galen urged, implying a literal meaning.

Galen knelt at the base of the door in search of a

---

[41] The erector spinae muscles represent a group of three muscles which include the iliocostalis, longissimus, and spinalis muscles. As its name implies, bilateral contraction of this muscle group causes the erection of the spine and, thus, the extension of the vertebral column.

safety release, but the entire latching mechanism was external. Despite a concerted effort with the flat bar, the shallow channel the door rested in would not permit a proper bite to gain a mechanical advantage. Recognizing their options were quickly fading, Tome summoned Cato over the walkie-talkie. The last bar of battery life blinked faster than a broken turn signal. "Mayday! Mayday!" Tome chanted.

"We read you loud and clear," answered Cato. "Where are you?"

"We're stuck in the box truck at the museum's loading dock!"

"We'r- s-ndin- -elp." Cato's voice cut out as the battery's remaining juice ran dry.

"Did you throw a dead body in here, Vince? I swear these crates are getting heavier," complained the stocky man in the gray jumpsuit. The movers arduously loaded the remaining empty crates onto their dollies and headed to the freight elevator. They rode the lift until they emerged onto the eighth floor.

"Oh! So sorry," blurted the elder guard as he stepped aside to make room for the moving crew exiting the questionable lift. The guard preferred to take the freight elevator to his car at the end of every shift because he liked its character. It reminded him of his time as a courier for an old warehouse used as a schoolbook depository. A wide grin grew on his face, accentuating his deep nasolabial folds and the crow's feet around his eyes. "Those must be for the plastinated bodies. It's too bad many of the specimens are leaving us." He held back the metal curtain. "Visitors are always fascinated to know what hides beneath their own physique," the guard added as he stepped into the elevator and disappeared behind the interwoven metal cage.

At the end of the corridor, both movers stopped and tipped their loads to the floor to ajar the exhibit doors. They opened the double doors in unison like waiters synchronously revealing a delectable presentation at a fine restaurant. The specimens stood stoically on their platforms. A few meters away, a strip of thin white napery lay on the marble floor as if someone's shoe had smuggled a strand of toilet paper from the restroom. "Look what Grandpa left behind," commented Vince with a chuckle, referencing the guard they had just encountered. The movers offloaded the crates.

Minutes passed, feeling like hours. Galen and Tome sat helplessly opposite one another on the truck's bed. Galen spun Morgan's bracelet around his fingers. The calming vibrations of the truck lulled Tome into a more peaceful state. His neck craned as the lambda of his skull[42] rested against the wall. "I never would have imagined this is how my second life would end," Tome said as his mind reticently recounted the night's events.

Galen reflected aloud, "I made a huge mistake. Arden was right. I acted with reckless abandon. This mission was too risky. I should have listened to him." Galen couldn't bear to look Tome in the eyes. "In the course of a single night, we've lost a friend at the hand of the

---

[42] The lambda of the skull is the point where the sagittal and lambdoid sutures of the skull unite. The sagittal suture runs in the midline and adjoins the two parietal bones. The curved lambdoid suture joins the occipital bone at the back of the skull to the parietal bones.

Code, failed at adding years onto Morgan's life, and now we find ourselves in a hopeless situation. This mission was a complete blunder."

"At least you were able to give Morgan a proper goodbye. And now that your past and present memories are entangled, you'll remember her indefinitely. That's something to cherish, don't you think?" Tome felt emphasizing positivity was better than taking a grudge with him to his second grave. "No other body in our world has ever been so fortunate. Your courage to do the unthinkable and your passion for helping others is reinvigorating." Tome's kind words floated to Galen like drifting cottonwood seeds.

Suddenly, the engine's low purring rumble went quiet. The oscillating vibrations of the truck's frame ceased. Seconds later, an audible thump of the truck's hood disrupted the subdued silence.

"Let's head out," rang the voice of one of the men in the drab gray jumpsuits. The doors of the truck's cab slammed shut one after the other like a drum flam. A buzzing sound replaced the chatter of the engine's ignition.

Without warning, the rolling door flung open. The head of a figure, wrapped in white linen strips, stared at them with laser beam eyes like a displeased wife scorning her husband. A shiver ran down Galen's spine as he looked into the oculi of a bonafide mummy with nickel dog tags hanging from its neck. The truck roared to life and lurched forward. "Let's go!" shouted a familiar voice. Without hesitation, Galen and Tome leaped from the truck's bed to the docking platform before the distance of the gap widened beyond their stride. After they regained their composure, the two met the figure face-to-face.

"This is the best I could do on such short notice," said the figure as he unwrapped the shroud of linen from his head. It was Arden.

"How did you evade the movers?" Tome asked, thrilled by Arden's rescue.

"The art of redirection," Arden stated. "I disconnected the truck's battery. While they tended to that, I unlatched the door."

With the box truck's door wide open, the exhaust left a plum of smog in the air as the truck sped away from the loading dock destined for the art museum over a mile away.

The truck circuitously winded across town, attempting to avoid the morning rush hour traffic. It aggressively dispersed water from sunken potholes, plowed over speed humps, and swerved past sluggish cars. The unsecured crate Galen had occupied waddled itself to the edge of the truck's back bumper where it teetered teasing to fall. A nudge from yet another pothole sent it tumbling to the pavement where it cracked like an egg loosening its ridged form. A sedan immediately trailing the truck swerved and braked to avoid the crate barreling toward its front end. Taillights lit up like a casino slot machine in a line of seven cars that rushed to avoid colliding.

Among the attentive drivers, Elena Floundary jerked forward in her seat as her seatbelt locked to restrain her. With the brake pedal pressed through the floorboard, she brought her car to a screeching stop without incident. Elana released a tightly held breath. She looked about to identify the cause of the abrupt standstill. Unable to make out the source of the delay several cars ahead, she suspected the blockage may not be short-lived. Hoping to return to the hospital before Jesse awoke, Elena's patience wore thin. As any anxious mother would, she cranked the steering wheel and swerved past a jeep occupying the oncoming traffic lane. She turned sharply onto the next available side street to circumvent the blockage.

Elena's unexpected detour took her past the Heidelberg Museum's grand entrance. At the pinnacle of a succession of stairs, two colorful larger-than-life banners hung suspended between stone columns commanding onlookers' attention. Each banner showcased the best of the Plastination Planet exhibit. The first read, *Discover What You're Made of*. Captivated by the pennants swaying in the wind, Elena depressed the brake sharply for a second time upon realizing the traffic light ahead beamed red. As her car idled at the light, Elena glanced back at the advertisements. "Wow, Jesse would love to see this," she thought to herself. On the second poster in smaller script, Elena read aloud, "*Accept death as part of life's journey.*"

CHAPTER 25

Until Next Time

Never had Galen or Tome seen the exhibit from the perspective of a visitor. Both were taken aback by the beauty of each specimen on display in their moritati poses.

"Thank you for saving us," Galen said to Arden, who tossed the linen wrappings in the waste receptacle next to him. "I'm sorry you had to get involved. I should have listened to you." Galen opened his bag and fished around until he located Arden's ID. "We won't be needing this anytime soon," commented Galen as he returned the badge to Arden. Arden tucked the badge into his lieutenant's jacket on his display platform.

Minutes before the museum officially opened, the others quickly gathered to welcome back Galen and Tome. Then Cameo asked the dreaded question, "Where's Marcel?"

Galen felt a lump form in his throat. He didn't want to recap Marcel's demise but knew he had to update the others on all that transpired throughout the evening. Tome nodded to Galen, indicating his support and willingness to fill in the details.

For the next few minutes, Galen chronicled their daring adventure. His recounting of the night's events was as engaging as a century-old fable brimming with action, heroic love, and tragic loss. He reminisced about the university's tunnel system, depicted their time in the cadaver lab, and told of his close encounter with Dr. Simon Floundary when trying to enter Morgan's name into the drug trial database. Then he paused. With his eyes angled to the marble floor, Galen described how Marcel gave his life, breaking the Code of Silence, to save the mission and a girl he had never met. Gasps of disbelief filled the room like heavy smog.

"You mean the Code of Silence is real? Cassius questioned.

"I always thought the Code was a scare tactic by the Council to prevent us from doing something stupid in public," Cameo admitted.

"I, too, had my doubts," added Cato.

"The Code is real and is essential for preserving the order between the living and the dead," interjected Arden with his usual authority.

Galen hesitantly concluded, "Unfortunately, Marcel's sacrifice was all in vain. I was not able to administer the Ribozore to Morgan." Deep down, he realized he should have heeded Arden's warning and left the natural order alone. "Morgan's fate is in the hands of a higher power now," accepted Galen as he looked away defeated.

Arden, in a respectful tone, intervened, "There is no

shame in failure. The only failure is not trying."

Tome hooked his arm around Galen's shoulders. "You didn't fail, Galen. Don't forget about this." Tome raised Morgan's bracelet for the others to see. Beams of light from above danced off the sparkling charms like splattering raindrops. Tome pressed the bracelet into Galen's palm and tightly closed Galen's fingers around it. "You have shown Morgan, and all of us, how to be the best of ourselves. You have reminded us of the value of tenacity. You have given us a renewed strength to confront unknowns with courage. You've taught us not to fear failure. You've shown us how our purpose impacts the living. Morgan will always be with you now. That is worth celebrating."

Clapping hands, from none other than Arden, broke the silence. The others raised their chins and joined in to recognize Galen for his commitment to Morgan and his awe-inspiring journey and to acknowledge Marcel's unyielding bravery and heroism.

"While I hate to cut this short, we must be mindful of the time," interjected an anxious Cassius. "The museum will open any minute now."

They all took their positions. At his platform, Galen placed Morgan's bracelet in his leather tote for safekeeping. He stood up to assume his moritati pose keeping his eyes fixated on the charm in the corner of his bag. At that moment, he knew Tome was right. Morgan would always be with him wherever he went.

The next time Galen opened his eyes, darkness enveloped him. He felt like a valuable heirloom tucked away in an impenetrable vault. He was unmistakably stowed in a wooden crate that smelled of Baltic birch. While excited for a new beginning, he was saddened he had not bid Arden farewell. His mind wandered as he dwelt on the impending unknowns. "Will Morgan ever receive the Ribozore? Is she going to be ok? Where is the exhibit relocating next? How many days do we have to be contained in these crates? Will I like the new museum? Wait, what if we're going to a storage facility instead of a new museum?" Galen shuttered at the thought of long-term confinement.

The clatter of unfastening latches distracted his worrisome thoughts. "That was a quick trip," Galen surmised to himself. Before he knew it, the crate's faceplate sprung open.

"Arden!" Galen blurted with delight. "I was worried I wasn't going to see you again. I didn't get to say goodbye. Have we arrived?" He peeked around Arden, realizing the answer was no. They were still in Heidelberg.

"Goodbyes always feel so permanent," said Arden. "As for you, your new journey begins tomorrow. What lies ahead will be hard work but rewarding. Once you've had this job for as long as I have, you'll learn to adapt your leadership style to the situation at hand. Whether you're a coach, visionary, or servant, always lead with your heart."

"When I have your job? Wait. What do you mean?" Galen asked perplexedly.

"I can't think of a better soldier to lead the others into the next chapter. As you know, I must stay behind to welcome our new cadre of bodies. I'm passing the torch to you, Galen. You were a source of light while living, and you've proven to spread that same luminescence even in death. And your new plastinate family cherishes your loyalty to the greater cause."

Galen was speechless. No words could describe how much Arden's words meant to him. "Thank you, Arden. I won't let you down."

Before closing Galen's crate, Arden removed one of the military pins from his jacket and pinned it on Galen's leather bag. Arden whispered something into Galen's ear and then stepped away. Arden gave a final valediction, "Until next time," as he repositioned the faceplate securely over the crate. Galen pressed his ear against the enclosure and listened until he could no longer hear Arden's sing-song humming. Galen's eyes glazed over as he fell back into a deep sleep.

CHAPTER 26

LUB-DUB

The previous night, after Mina returned home from the hospital, Morgan's little brother Spencer wrapped his arms so tightly around his mother's thigh that she felt she was wearing a full-legged cast. A glossy film saturated Mina's eyes as she absorbed his warmth and sincere affection.

Since the accident and Morgan's rehospitalization, Mina's parents had stepped in to care for Spencer. Though days measured the time in between, it felt like weeks since Mina had spent quality time with her son. Mina sensed that Spencer felt a bit like an orphan in his own family. Morgan, confined to the hospital bed, was not there to keep him company or help him pass the time. Mina was so preoccupied with Morgan and helping with Gavin's funeral that Spencer never fully received the attention and extra comfort he needed. Mina, now realizing the toll the last several days had taken on Spencer, promised her son a day fully devoted to him.

Mina was very proud of her handsome little guy, who had been so brave and strong amidst the last-minute changes. For a six-year-old, Mina felt he had demonstrated more courage and understanding than most adults. She could not fathom what he was experiencing. Now with Gavin gone, Spencer lost yet another male idol in his life. Since the death of Spencer's and Morgan's father, Gavin stepped in to support the family wherever he could, and, over time, became a role model to Spencer, despite always hanging out with his older sister.

Spencer and Gavin were two peas in a pod. Spencer was the little brother Gavin never had and Gavin was the big brother Spencer never had. They often got each other into trouble. Some weekends, when Gavin babysat, Spencer would pull harmless antics on Morgan, oftentimes with Gavin's prodding, while she ran errands with her mother. The night Spencer placed a live garden snake in Morgan's pillowcase to get a rouse out of her solidified his place as the family prankster. Despite his fiendish schemes, Spencer had a heart of compassion. Mina could tell he dearly missed Gavin and anxiously longed for Morgan's return home.

"First thing in the morning, let's find some costumes to wear to the Cologne Carnival. What do you say?" Mina suggested to Spencer. Every year, the Lowe family made it a point to embody the spirit of the carnival season. Though, Mina and the kids were always more enthusiastic about it than their father. Over the years, the elaborate costumes and excessive fanfare became too eccentric for their father's liking.

"Will Morgan be able to come with us to the carnival?" Spencer asked with excitement, hoping for some sense of normalcy.

"I'm afraid not," Mina replied. "Morgan will likely be in the hospital for several more days until her heart gets a little stronger. Maybe we can bring her back a special gift. And one for Grandma Lowe, too, for staying with her."

"Okay," Spencer sighed, knowing it was how it had to be.

At the Rialto the next morning, Spencer selected a classic tyrannosaurus rex ensemble complete with an elongated tail, tiny upper limbs, and impressive razor-sharp foam teeth. Mina conceded to the theme and selected attire fitting for a prehistoric cavewoman.

When they returned home, Spencer assisted Mina with every accumulated chore. He did not want to leave his mother's side. He changed the laundry and vacuumed the family room carpet without his mother ever asking. When Mina asked Spencer to take a few items to the recycling basket in the garage, Spencer cowered, fearful that Gavin's dirt bike would evoke a flood of unwelcome emotions. Because the Lowe's house backed up to a large forest preserve, Gavin stored his dirt bike in their garage so it would be on hand whenever he felt the urge to ride wild and free. Noticing his hesitancy and realizing the weight of her innocent request, Mina quickly interceded. "Never mind, I'll take care of it," Mina said nonchalantly, hoping Spencer would not dwell on the thought.

Spencer sat quietly on the couch as Mina passed by returning from the garage. His head hung low as he stared into the black void of an empty iPad screen.

"Come on, kiddo, will you help me with the dishes? Then we'll make bratwursts with noodles for dinner. Your favorite!" Mina said in a peppy voice, trying to shake Spencer from his lull. Spencer dramatically rolled off the couch, as any six-year-old boy would, and pulled up a kitchen chair alongside his mother to help rinse and dry the dishes. His eye roll said it all.

Mina's cell phone buzzed. She did not bother to look at the caller-ID. She assumed it was her sister who often called in the afternoon on her drive home from work. She quickly dried one hand with a nearby dish towel and snuggly pinched the phone in the crook of her neck.

"Hello, Mrs. Lowe," said a calm voice on the other end of the line. "This is Morgan's cardiologist." Mina's stomach sank in her abdomen. Astonished by the call's unexpectedness, Mina's heart fluttered as she nearly dropped her cell phone in the soapy dishwater.

"I'm calling to inform you that a pediatric heart just became available. With Morgan's advanced cardiomyo-pathy, she is a prime candidate for the heart. If you accept the donation, we would like to give Morgan a final evaluation and prepare her for surgery, assuming she meets all the requirements." Hearing no response from Mina, the cardiologist continued. "Per our protocol, we'll take a blood sample to ensure Morgan is free of infection and that she has a clear toxicology report. The donor's heart is only viable for about four hours. If you provide us with your verbal consent now, we'll begin the process and will have you sign the documentation when you arrive at the hospital."

"Yes. Yes, of course. I give my full consent," Mina blurted without giving it a second thought. The lub-dub of Mina's heart raced faster than an up-tempo song marked *presto*. As she felt her own heart sprinting within her middle mediastinum, Mina chilled at the thought of Morgan's God-given heart being intentionally arrested and replaced.

"Quickly run upstairs and pack a bag," Mina ordered Spencer. "Your sister is getting a new heart!"

Spencer dutifully followed his mother's instructions, excited at the prospect of his sister being healthy again. Maybe for once they could both be treated like normal children, free to run and play at will with unsupervised independence. Not knowing how soon he would see Morgan again, he packed his favorite deck of magic cards. He wanted to be ready at any moment to impress her with the new trick he had learned.

When they arrived at the hospital, Mina and Spencer walked with a purpose through the building's front entrance. All that was on Mina's mind was her need to see her baby girl one last time before the staff carted her to the operating room. As an intensive care nurse, Mina knew the risks associated with open-heart surgery. It took all that she could muster to block the facts from her thoughts. As the two passed the information desk in the hospital's lobby, Mina gave a nod of acknowledgment to the attendants who came to know her by name over the many years of checkups and changes to Morgan's medication regimens. For Mina, this encounter was different. It was substantive. It held the promise of being life changing.

The elevator doors sprung open on cue as if waiting for Mina and Spencer to arrive. A somber couple exited. The woman's head was downcast, and her eyelids drooped like heavy curtains. Lacrimal secretions left streaks of mascara beneath her long flowing eyelashes, something Mina knew all too well. The man who accompanied the fragile woman wore a hickory brown jacket embossed with the national emblem on the shoulder. Mina enjoyed the pleasantness of the man's strong scented cologne. The familiar-looking gentleman wrapped his arm tightly around the woman in a comforting demeanor, like a child cuddling his favorite comfort object. He rubbed his eyes as if to erase the inflamed capillaries of his bloodshot sclera.[43] Mina speculated about their grief. The couple, spellbound by devastation, never saw Mina or Spencer pass by.

Amelia Lowe waited for Mina and Spencer just outside of Morgan's hospital room. "Grandma!" Spencer exclaimed, always excited to see her.

"You're just in time. They're almost ready to take her," Amelia remarked to Mina.

Acknowledging her mother-in-law, Mina rushed into the room. There were so many nurses and doctors, Mina could not establish a clear line of sight with her daughter. The hospital staff stepped aside like magnets repelling their opposing forces. At Morgan's bedside,

---

[43] The sclera is the tough white outer layer of the eyeball that helps to maintain the shape of the eye.

Mina clasped her daughter's hand in her own.

"Don't worry, Mom. I'll be fine," said Morgan, comforting her mother before her mother had a chance to console her. "Hey, bud!" Morgan expressed with a smile upon seeing her little brother for the first time since the accident. Spencer awkwardly hugged Morgan's leg while she sat reclined in the Fowler's position.

"Morgan's bloodwork came back clear," interjected her cardiologist. "The cardiovascular surgeon is standing by. We're ready when you are."

"We will all be praying that everything goes well. You are such a strong young woman. I know you will make it through this," Mina recited to Morgan.

"See you in recovery, Mom," Morgan replied with a tight smile stretching across her small pale face. Mina savored the words, hoping they would soon become reality.

Mina lowered her ear to Morgan's chest. Lub-dub, lub-dub, lub-dub, faintly called the valves of Morgan's weak and dying heart. The lub, the S1 heart sound, was softer than that of a healthy patient due to her left ventricle's decreased contractility. The severity of Morgan's cardiomyopathy was undeniable, from her physically swollen appearance to her heightened fatigue. "I love you so much, honey. Don't ever forget that," whispered Mina.

A nurse hovering nearby latched the bed rails on either side of Morgan to secure her for transport. "She's in good hands," the nurse reassured.

Spencer reached through one of the bed rails and laid his small delicate hand on top of Morgan's where an IV catheter had been inserted. Instead of noticeably wincing in pain, Morgan gritted her teeth and touched Spencer with one finger on his forearm, "Got ya last, little buddy."

The staff wheeled Morgan down the hallway through a set of swinging double doors. Just like Spencer's magic trick he had yet to show her, Morgan was there one moment and gone the next.

Mina stood expressionless in the center of the cardiac unit, not knowing whether to cry out of fear or for joy. Spencer brushed up alongside his mother. He held tight to his deck of magic cards in one hand and cradled Mina's hand in the other.

CHAPTER 27

HEAVEN'S ANGELS

The air was more humid than usual for a late summer day. The cloud-laden sky cast a dim sleepy hue over the city and its neighboring hillsides. Though the weather was not at its peak of beauty, Morgan's spirit was thriving.

Morgan sat upright in her hospital bed with her legs crossed underneath her. The profuse swelling in her lower limbs had finally resided, allowing her to sit as she desired for the first time since arriving back in the cardiac unit. She felt strong enough to take a walk through the hospital's courtyards but knew her mother would disapprove.

Spencer sat at the end of the same hospital bed facing Morgan with a deck of cards in hand. "Watch carefully," he insisted as he laid five cards out in front of her one by one on the white bed sheet. "You're going to be amazed." He could hardly contain his excitement. Spencer had practiced the card trick tirelessly and waited patiently for days to demonstrate his new skills to his big sister. He was more than ready to convince Morgan that he could read her mind and reveal the exact card she was thinking of. His sleight of hand was practically flawless, for a six-year-old at least. The big reveal was spot on. Morgan expressed amazement with an extra oomph of elation, knowing it was exactly what Spencer needed.

Morgan's lead cardiologist, Dr. Ziegler, entered the room to check in. "All of your discharge paperwork is complete. You have a clean bill of health and are free to go," he uttered in a cheerful voice, genuinely excited for his patient's return home. As soon as the doctor declared Morgan healthy enough to leave, a nurse assisted her into a waiting wheelchair. To Morgan, the wheelchair felt like a golden chariot, gallantly escorting her to the start of her new worry-free life. Beyond the door of her hospital room, a sea of doctors, nurses, respiratory therapists, medical trainees, and volunteers lined the unit's main corridor all the way to the elevators. When Morgan's wheelchair broke the doorway's threshold, a swell of applause, cheers, and whistling lifted her and transported Morgan through the aisle of caretakers like a fluffy cumulonimbus cloud carrying one of heaven's angels. Morgan's grandiose exit perfectly symbolized her incredible triumph over a condition that plagued her since early childhood. Morgan's spirits were as high as they had ever been. She knew there was only one way for her to celebrate.

Mina started the car's ignition with the press of a button. "What's the first thing you plan to do when you get home," Mina asked, anticipating her daughter would want to invite Paige over for an afternoon of manicures and trivial chitchat.

"Can we stop somewhere first?" asked Morgan from the backseat, as if a side excursion before returning home was important to her.

"I suppose," replied Mina glancing at Morgan in the rearview mirror, her eyes squinting baffled by her daughter's timbre. "What did you have in mind?"

"I would like to get some ice cream."

"I don't think that's a good idea, Morgan."

"If Gavin was here to celebrate with us, the ice cream parlor would be our first stop," insisted Morgan.

Recognizing all that Morgan had missed out on in the days that followed the accident, Mina's heart gave in to help her daughter find closure. On approach, Mina shuttered at the sight of *Harold's Ice Cream Café*. The patio tables and chairs mangled by the incident were absent, leaving a noticeable void near the sidewalk. The trunk of a nearby sapling snapped at knee level was the only visible remnant of the wreck. Mina held her breath as she escorted her children to the counter to place their orders.

Morgan ordered Gavin's favorite, a brownie delight with vanilla ice cream and a dollop of whipped cream. Spencer opted for an ice cream sandwich. Mina's stomach was tied in so many knots she had no appetite. Much to Mina's dismay, the three were forced to sit outdoors at a black wrought iron table to consume their sweet treats.

At a neighboring table, Morgan noticed a tricolored border collie laying to the side of his owner with his leash wrapped around the chair's legs. The collie's face was beautifully speckled with symmetric patches of black, white, and caramel fur. The pup's dove white paws complimented his mostly black coat and white trimmed underbelly. Two overly boisterous and chatty women were seated at the neighboring table. Each enjoyed a hearty scoop of mint chocolate chip ice cream. The woman with her back closest to Morgan wore an olive cardigan and could be heard emphatically recounting her family's weekend fanfare.

"I found the entire experience grotesque, but at the same time there was something surreal about it." The dame's odd yet intriguing statement drew Morgan in as she gravitated closer to improve her eves dropping while placing the napkins on the table.

"I can't decide if I would ever want to see the exhibit. Paying an entrance fee to walk among the dead isn't my idea of a good time. What was your favorite part?" asked the other woman whose bouncing bobbed haircut was just as distracting as her nasal voice. She held her cold treat in one hand and her phone in the other. She was clearly the multitasking type.

The woman in the cardigan pondered with her face still hidden from view. As Morgan lowered herself to take her seat, the dim-witted woman responded, "They were so life-like. The muscles on their dissected faces were so delicate." Morgan nearly fell from her chair as the cardigan woman's description triggered a flashback of her unannounced early morning visitor. Morgan's new heart fluttered so violently she could not help but raise her hand to her chest. The woman's voice trailed off as Morgan became consumed by her thoughts.

"That's impossible," Morgan uttered under her breath, "It defies the laws of nature."

"Are you alright Morgan? You look like you've seen a ghost," said Mina. "Do we need to take you back to the hospital?"

"No, Mom! I'm fine," Morgan replied. "I'm just a little frazzled. I think this fresh air and some more walking will do me some good. Maybe we could do something fun soon, …like go to a museum."

"That would be fun," Mina replied as she and Spencer took their seats at the table. Vanilla ice cream already lined the corners of Spencer's mouth. "But I think you need to build up your endurance first."

"You're disgusting!" Morgan barked at Spencer as she pointed to his dirty face.

"See, Mom, she's back to her normal self," sneered Spencer.

"That's enough," scolded Mina. "You're lucky to have each other. Would you rather be separated for months on end again?"

"No," both Morgan and Spencer grouched in unison, though their reply was drowned out by the two women's vexing cackles.

"Is Gavin with Daddy and heaven's angels now?" Spencer innocently asked, while licking the center of his ice cream-filled cookie.

"That's right," Mina answered, peering over to Morgan to see her response to Spencer's comment.

Morgan chimed in, "I think God has given Gavin a very special assignment."

"Maybe he's helping CIA operatives," Spencer suggested.

"And from where exactly did you learn about spies?" Mina asked, bewildered by her son's knowledge of government infiltrants.

"I've watched a lot of television recently," remarked Spencer.

Morgan speculated herself, "No, I think Gavin's assignment is even more important than helping CIA operatives. I think he's helping people to be the best of themselves and to realize their own potential."

"What gives you that idea?" interjected Mina.

"I just know."

CHAPTER 28

MANIFEST

Amazement stunned Galen. "Wow! Look at all those windows," he said to Cameo as both admired the contemporary museum's beauty. From the middle of the sterile white gallery, they observed the roofline's contours cutting across the museum like rolling waves.

"I could get used to this. What an upgrade," Cameo replied as he echoed Galen's awe of the new building.

The gallery overlooked a mirror pond flanked by grassy knolls and well-manicured landscaping. The underlighting of the eastern redbud trees and sugar maples complimented the path lights of a meandering flagstone walkway. At the center of the pond, an illuminated fountain commanded onlookers' attention with a focal geyser surrounded by a spraying crown of water.

A cluttered accumulation of boxes, crates, and packaging wrap detracted from the main gallery's picturesque view. Knowing the onslaught of tasks ahead, Galen went straight to the crate manifest to begin taking inventory. He quickly flipped through the stack of papers attached to the clipboard to gauge his evening's workload. Much to his surprise, hidden under the last page of the manifest, he found a handwritten note penned in permanent marker on the clipboard's face.

"Face your new world and responsibilities with confidence and vigor. Always lead with your heart. From you will come great things," read the message, signed — Arden. Galen stood humbled, feeling inadequate and undeserving of his new role.

"Good evening, boss. How may I be of service?" spoke Cassius in a cheerful voice.

"We must first take a census to ensure we've left no one behind," said Galen with conviction. "For efficiency's sake, as we do rounds, we can begin to configure the displays."

Galen and Cassius strolled throughout the gallery working in tandem. They took inventory and brought order to the most disheveled displays they encountered. Otis, Otto, and Ivan were already gambling in a poker game as Galen and Cassius passed by. Galen paused briefly to study the game. Ivan had only five poker chips remaining, and the night was still young. From Galen's position, he overheard Otto declare, "Ivan, you must love origami because you're always folding." Ivan gave a stonewall expression while Otis and Otto snickered.

Out of Otis's and Otto's view, Galen covertly moved Nila's mirror into position across from the poker table in Ivan's line of sight. Next, he positioned the rack of organs, originally in the jazz club storeroom, at an angle several feet away from the mirror. He moved the small fetus in the Kilner jar to the row second from the top. With Galen's back to Ivan, all Ivan could see was Galen signing hand gestures to the developing fetus. Galen turned around, looked at Ivan straight in the orbits, and gave a thumb's up. Ivan, confused by Galen's signal, cocked his skull. As Galen moved on to continue his inventory, Ivan remained fixed on the fetus. Like a street vendor dancing with a sign to attract the attention of gawkers, the fetus began signaling in the direction of the mirror. Ivan glanced over. Otis's poker hand was as visible as the letter "E" at an optometrist's office. Ivan grinned with a slight deviation of his mandible. He peered back at the fetus. It was Otto's turn at the table. This time, the fetus pantomimed Otto's bluff. Ivan now had the full advantage.

Over the next hour, Ivan made an unlikely comeback to win his first-ever poker game. Otis and Otto exchanged grumbles as they stomped away from the velvet-lined octagonal table to blow off steam. With their heads hung low, Otis and Otto animatedly flailed their limbs in pure chagrin. Galen chuckled from a distance.

After three full hours, Galen and Cassius marked off the last checkbox of the manifest. "That's it. We've accounted for everyone and everything," said Galen, feeling a sense of accomplishment. Though the displays' layouts were different from before, the gallery teemed with life. The uptick in laughter and the commotion of the bodies' typical activities was evidence of acclimation.

Galen and Cassius sat on Galen's platform for a much-needed break. Galen smiled with delight as the ostrich scurried in front of them with Vitalis trailing in hot pursuit. As they reflected on their work, Cassius obsessively peered at a crate at the edge of the gallery. An alphanumeric code inscribed the top rim of all cargo that came from Heidelberg. As Cassius gazed at the unidentified crate, he grew concerned they had missed one.

"What's the matter?" Galen inquired of Cassius.

"Did we record an entry for that crate in the corner?"

"Let's double-check." The curious duo walked to the unidentified crate and gave it a careful inspection. "You're right! It has no shipping code, and it hasn't been opened." Galen checked his clipboard. "The crate is not on the manifest."

-- Dot, dot, da-dot dot -- Cassius knocked on the side of the crate and waited for a response.

Nothing.

-- Dot...dot -- the crate responded timidly, returning two knocks.

Galen and Cassius exchanged glances of curiosity. "Stand back! We're going to pry open the crate," Galen called to the inhabitant.

Cassius, already a step ahead, held out a rib spreader from a thoracotomy tray. "Maybe this will work. It came in this box with the crate."

With no other options available, Galen agreed, "Let's give it a try."

Galen jammed the retractor between the frame and the front panel. He turned the crank of the spreader inch-by-inch until the plank separated from the frame. As the gap widened, Galen inserted his hands at the container's top and continued to pry. Cassius, with good intentions, bent over to pry the bottom of the encasement but his drawers slipped from their slots and clattered to the ground. Embarrassed, Cassius scampered after his drawers like a child chasing a set of loose marbles.

A reverberating giggle emerged from inside the crate. The inhabitant saw Cassius's fumble through the crate's newly formed crevice. Finally, the crate opened like the crisp pop of a pickle jar. Galen and Cassius peered into the wooden box. A shy adolescent male sat nestled in the corner with his forearms wrapped tightly around his knees.

Immediately, Galen recalled his first day in the exhibit and sympathized with the boy. After contemplating what Arden would do, Galen nudged Cassius out of view to the container's side and followed suit himself. Though the boy could no longer see him, Galen crouched closer to his level. A faint reflection of the boy could be seen in the glass window opposite the crate.

"My name is Galen. What's yours?" he said, hoping to provide comfort through casual conversation.

After no response, Galen tried again. "We're nothing to be afraid of. We may look a little different and strange, but we're here to help you." After a pregnant pause, Galen continued, "If you come out of the case, we'll explain everything. Don't be frightened. It's okay," Galen encouraged in a tender reassuring voice.

In the reflection, Galen saw the boy bashfully rise to his feet. As he stood, the midline of his chest glistened. A titanium wire wrapped his sternum in a tight descending spiral. A precise and intentional fracture ran from his manubrium[44] to his xiphoid process.

The boy emerged cautiously from the crate. "I'm Jesse," he replied with his eyes fixed on Galen's and Cassius's reflections.

Galen stood and stepped forward to face the boy. He extended his hand in solidarity. "Hi, Jesse. I'm Galen. I hope you and I can become good friends."

"That's strange," Cassius said aloud. "Your nameplate also reads *Jesse*, which means *gift of God* in Hebrew."

"You must be some special gift," Galen surmised with a nod of his brow. The very moment Galen clutched the boy's hand, a surge of extreme warmth and comfort overwhelmed Galen's body as he connected with Jesse. "I have a new world to show you...and you have much to learn. Follow me."

---

[44] The sternum (breastbone) resembles the shape of a sword and is divided into three parts including the manubrium (Latin for "handle"), body, and xiphoid process (the tip of the sword).

THE PLASTINATION PROCESS

Plastination was invented by Dr. Gunther von Hagens in 1977 and is a method for indefinitely preserving tissues and anatomical specimens. The entire preparation and plastination process involves six steps and takes approximately one year from start to finish for every specimen (see table below). For more information on the plastination process and plastinated specimens visit vonhagens-plastination.com.

Completion Time	Fixation, Dissection, and Plastination Process
3-4 hours	**FIXATION** prevents the decomposition of donated tissues by killing bacteria with Formaldehyde and other preservation solutions.
2-3 months	**DISSECTION** is the process of fully, clearly, and cleanly exposing anatomical structures by removing the skin, fat, and connective tissues. The time required for this step varies depending on the complexity of both the specimen and the dissection being performed.
2-3 months	**DEHYDRATION** involves removing water and dissolving fats by submerging the specimen in an acetone bath. With the temperature of the acetone at -13°F (-25°C), the acetone draws out and replaces the water in the specimen's cells.

1-2 months	**FORCED IMPREGNATION** involves submerging the specimen in a liquid polymer (e.g., silicone) bath. Under a vacuum, the acetone boils and vaporizes. As the acetone leaves the cells, it is replaced by the liquid polymer. Upon completion of this step, the specimen is still very flexible.
1-2 months	**POSITIONING** the body into the desired pose requires the use of wires, needles, clamps, and foam blocks.
2-3 months	**CURING** is the final step whereby either gas, light, or heat (depending on the polymer) is used to harden the specimen. The curing process protects the plastinated specimen against decomposition and decay, thereby preserving it indefinitely.
1 year	Average total time to completion.

ACKNOWLEDGMENTS

With deepest gratitude, thank you to my supportive family and the individuals who reviewed and provided feedback on drafts of this novel. Thank you to my wife, Megan, my children, Mackenzie and Hank, my parents, Rodger and Kimberly Wilson, my sister, Hannah Anderson and her family, my in-laws, John and Marlene Jurca, and my sisters-in-law and their families, Kathryn Amundson and Kristen Jurca.

This novel was further improved through the help of teen reviewers who are the daughters of my close and trusted anatomy colleagues, Drs. Christopher Ferrigno and William Brooks. Thank you, Mia Ferrigno and Shelby Brooks for your thoughtful comments and help in further refining this book so that it can inspire future generations of prospective scientists to develop a passion for anatomy and the medical sciences.

Adam B. Wilson

A special thanks to those who gave their time to read and provide thoughtful feedback on our manuscript. These include my husband, Ricky Hansen, my parents, Ken and Francine Daemicke, and close family members.

Your honesty, suggestions, and advice helped us to refine our ideas and approach throughout the creative process. This book is richer thanks to your contributions.

Alexandra K. Daemicke

Collectively, we wish to thank Adam Jones, Ph.D., for his writing expertise and high-yield feedback that helped to steer this project in the right direction. Adam's excellent suggestions and coaching were highly pivotal in making this project a success.

Finally, the concept of this book and the learning of anatomy would be impossible if it were not for the altruistic gift of whole-body donors. Thank you to all donors, past, present, and future, for bequeathing your bodies for the furtherment of education and science.

AUTHOR BIOGRAPHIES

ADAM B. WILSON, Ph.D., is an associate professor of anatomy and the Director of Anatomy Education at Rush University in Chicago, Illinois. Dr. Wilson teaches gross anatomy to students in the health sciences and medical professions, conducts medical education research, and serves as an Associate Editor for the academic journal *Anatomical Sciences Education*. Adam lives in a suburb of Chicago with his wife and two children. Outside of his professorial role, Adam spends quality time with his family, is a praise band member at his church, and feeds his creativity through woodworking. Through the medium of creative storytelling, Adam hopes to embolden young minds to explore the allure of anatomy and the medical sciences.

ALEXANDRA K. DAEMICKE, M.S., is a Biological Sciences faculty member at the University of Illinois at Chicago. She has a graduate degree in human anatomical sciences and currently teaches biology-related courses to undergraduate students. Alexandra met Dr. Wilson as a graduate student, and their collective desire to share the beauty of the human body with others gave rise to collaborating on this novel.

WHY THIS BOOK WAS WRITTEN

In 2020, my research colleagues and I discovered a severe shortage of doctorally prepared anatomists within the United States. Our data, sourced through the National Science Foundation, revealed that over the past 51 years (1969-2019) the number of Ph.D. graduates in anatomy declined by 3.1 graduates per year reaching an all-time low of only eight graduates in 2017. The near extinction of trained anatomists comes at a time when academic healthcare programs and student enrollments are expanding to offset a potential shortage of as many as 124,000 physicians by the year 2034 as predicted by the Association of American Medical Colleges; thereby necessitating a higher demand for anatomy educators. Collectively, these findings revealed an opportunity and need to promote the anatomy profession to the next generation in a new and lively way. Ergo, *Cadaver Chronicles: The Code of Silence* was conceived as a medium for inspiring young minds to explore the bliss of anatomy and medicine through the melding of anatomical facts with science fantasy.

Anatomical sciences are often considered the cornerstone of medicine and classically include the study of gross anatomy, embryology, histology, and neuroanatomy. Gross anatomy is the study of organs, structures, and tissues that are visible to the naked eye. This ever-green discipline is taught by dedicated anatomy educators who are trained in the biomedical sciences and commonly hold a doctor of philosophy degree (Ph.D.). The teaching of gross anatomy relies on a combination of digital resources, anatomical models, illustrations, medical imaging (e.g., x-rays, CTs, MRI, ultrasound), and cadaveric dissections/prosections. The act of cadaveric dissection is a true privilege and has withstood the test of time as an invaluable method for learning the art and science of anatomy.

May those who read this book be inspired to deepen their understanding of the human form and perhaps one day pursue a career that applies anatomical knowledge to help advance the cause of science and medicine.

Adam B. Wilson, Ph.D.